HEAVEN IN A WILD FLOWER — TALE OF AN ANGLO-SAXON LEATHER-WORKER ON LINDISFARNE

ST CUTHBERT TRILOGY, BOOK 1

JOHN BROUGHTON

IN PRINCIPIO ERAT UERBUM
ET UERBUM ERAT APUD DM̄
ET D̄S ERAT UERBUM
HOC ERAT IN PRINCIPIO APUD DM̄
OMNIA PER IPSUM FACTA SUNT
ET SINE IPSO FACTUM EST NIHIL
QUOD FACTUM EST INIPSO UITAERAT̄
ET UITA ERAT LUX HOMINUM
ET LUX IN TENEBRIS LUCET
ET TENEBRAE EAM NON CON PRE
  HENDERUNT
FUIT HOMO MISSUS AD̄O
  CUI NOMEN ERAT IOHANNES
HIC UENIT IN TESTIMONIUM
UT TESTIMONIUM PER HIBERET
  DE LUMINE

Heaven in a Wild Flower is dedicated to my charming wife,
Maria Valente

ACKNOWLEDGMENTS

Special thanks go to my dear friend John Bentley for his steadfast and indefatigable support. His content checking and suggestions have made an invaluable contribution to
  Heaven in a Wild Flower.

Frontispiece is by Dawn Burgoyne, with the text a fragment from Folio 1 of St Cuthbert's Gospels (British Library). The illuminated capital is based on a border design from The Book of Durrow (Trinity College, Dublin)'.

Dawn Burgoyne, medieval re-enactor/presenter specialising in period scripts. Visit her on Facebook at dawnburgoynepresents.

ONE

HEXHAM, BERNICIA, APRIL 684 AD

WHAT I EVER WANTED TO DO WAS FOLLOW IN MY FATHER'S footsteps to be a leather-worker. In this, I largely succeeded except for a turbulent period that began in the workshop when a heavy hand laid on my shoulder made me start. I had just a score of winters behind me.

"Aella, son of Oswin?" a gruff voice said.

I put my knife on the bench and, although I am tall, looked up into the craggy features of a warrior a head taller than I.

"I am Aella, but who are you?"

"My name is Berhtred and I am here on King Ecgfrith's business. You and your father are to come with me to war.

My heart leapt in my chest— unlike father, I had never been into battle.

"Where is Oswin?"

At last, he released the strong grip on my shoulder, at the same time pulling me round to face him. His broad chest, slim belted waist and muscled thighs told me he was as fit as a moorland stag; therefore, not a man to contradict. But that is what I had to do.

"Father cannot come, he lies abed with a sickness these five days. And if he is sick, who is to carry on the workshop if not I?"

He added a frown to his graven countenance and his hand went to the hilt of his seax.

"Would you defy your king, lad?"

I gulped, tried to force a smile and said,

"I will take you to father, Lord. You shall see for yourself how he fares and I obey his every word. Perhaps you will tell him of the king's command?"

For one foolish moment, I thought of grabbing my knife, so close to hand, but the sheer size of the man and his undoubted prowess in a fight cooled my ardour.

"I will lead the way, Lord."

The house needed a change of air because it was smoky and stuffy but my mother would not allow any draughts to worsen father's fever.

"Mother, this is Lord Berhtred. He must speak with my sire."

She looked anxiously at the towering figure, "But my husband is unwell, Lord."

The warrior smiled grimly, "Fear not, mistress. I come on the king's order and I will not overtax your man."

I felt sure that he was checking on the honesty of my words, although what the haggard woman in front of him had just said should have been a confirmation. She pulled aside a heavy drape and indicated the space beyond that served as their bedroom. Father lay pale on his pallet, his brow glistening due to the fever. He groaned and tried to sit up but a huge hand pressed him down and considerately tugged the sheepskin back over his chest.

"I am sorry you are unwell, Master Oswin. King Ecgfrith sent me to gather men. We are away to war and the village

2

headman gave me your name and that of Aella. It is clear to me that you are in no condition to rise from your sickbed, but your son is hale and will serve our purpose."

I heard mother gasp and father's eyes moved anxiously from our visitor to me. He looked aghast but could only groan.

"Are we to starve?" mother wailed, "Who will work the leather?"

The poor woman asked my earlier question. Without finished articles to barter for food, she would be in dire circumstances.

"If all goes well, Mistress, your son will be home before the autumn and his purse will bulge after his service.

This thought heartened me, but I had never fought in earnest and decided to use this as my final ploy.

"Lord, I am happy to do the king's bidding but I am no warrior. I scarcely know how to wield an axe."

A deep throaty laugh boomed in the confined space.

"There will be time for that, fine fellow. Come here, let me feel your muscles."

He grabbed my arm and squeezed as I clenched my fist and raised it.

"You are no weakling, lad. We'll soon have you ready. Master Oswin, I will send you a healer forthwith, but you are excused the summons. I bid you both farewell. You, Aella, come with me!

What choice did I have? Back in the village, I was delighted when he pressed Edwy the miller's son into service. As children and youths, we had been inseparable. Work had caused us to drift apart except at feasts and ceremonies when we sought each other. Having an old friend on this venture, whatever it was, made a huge difference to my mood.

Berhtred was a man of his word: one of his few saving

graces. He took us back to the chief, Hrodgar, and pressed silver coins into his hand.

"Find a healer for Master Oswin. When I come back to your village, I wish to see him on his feet and working his leather. Understand?"

His voice was generally gruff, but the last word was loaded with menace.

Hrodgar gazed from the money in his hand to the rugged face of the warrior.

"It is quite clear, Lord, I know just the woman. I'll send a boy to fetch her forthwith."

"Good, see you do! If Master Oswin is not cured, I'll know who to blame."

Our headman was formidable, used to bullying and getting his way, but he knew when to be subservient.

"The wise woman is skilled and will set Oswin to rights."

I glared at Hrodgar, for he had given my name to the intimidating giant who was now steering us out of the hall.

"My thanks, for the healer, Lord," I said.

He looked down at me,

"You will repay me with good and faithful service, Aella!"

In this matter, I had no choice.

The three of us set off along the trail that took us into the depths of the forest. Edwy and I knew the woodlands from boyhood and even now I came here in search of food. Young boars were my favourite prey but one had to be careful of the fury and vengeance of the adult beasts.

Little sunlight penetrated the canopy, despite it being springtime. The thicker summer foliage was more impenetrable but the April sky was grey today and the sun weak, so I couldn't judge the time. I reckon we'd been marching for two hours and I began to feel weary when the clamour of voices drifted on the breeze.

"We are here," was all Berhtred said.

'Here' turned out to be a large clearing by a stream. The tree-fringed dell was full of tents where men were sitting around fires, laughing and drinking. The nearest group fell silent when Berhtred drew near and looked anxiously up at him. He grasped one of them and hauled him to his feet,

"Shift your stumps, Sibbald. I want these men to be fitted out with weapons and armour.

"Ay, Lord."

He rubbed his arm and I sympathised; my shoulder still ached from his earlier grip. The man led us to a billowing tent near the centre of the enclosure. Brushing aside the linen flap, he ducked inside and bade us follow. He opened a large chest and was pulling out leather breastplates. My expertise told me they were tough and made of ox hide. It was a relief that we wouldn't be wearing mail shirts because these were much lighter and would protect from a seax blade if not a powerful spear thrust. Sibbald had a good eye or an experienced one because the sizes were perfect. Next, he passed greaves of the same material to shield our legs. Then, he said,

"Now young 'un," addressing me, "Will you take an axe or a sword?"

I had no hesitation. I'd never once wielded a sword, but used an axe to chop wood for the fire. This weapon was much heftier and I looked at it dubiously,

"Are there any axemen to teach me?"

He grinned,

"Don't worry about that, Berhtred the Butcher will soon knock you into shape, my lad."

I still wonder if it was that remark that made Edwy choose a sword. If so, he had chosen the harder school, as it later ensued.

"That'll do for now," Sibbald said, "the javelins and spears are still in untied bundles."

"Where are we headed?" I asked.

"Nobody's quite sure. Berhtred's still picking up men or *boys*, like you two," he sneered.

I promised myself I'd make him rue those words if I ever got the chance, but kept my own counsel for the moment. It was just as well because I soon grew to like him, beginning with his offer for us to join him by the fire to sup ale.

Over a drink, he confided in a low voice,

"Some say we're heading overseas, but I can't rightly say."

"But where would that be? Frankia? Ériu?" I had heard them named but knew nought of their whereabouts.

He looked puzzled. I think we'll be here for some days yet. The lads are guessing because someone heard Berhtred say we're waiting for the good weather to come. That won't be for at least a month. Berhtred will have you training in the mornings, like the rest of us, and resting up in the afternoons until we move out. You'll be proper warriors by then. There's sure to be other recruits coming from the lands around here. I'm surprised he only brought two from your village."

"It's a small place, four or five farmsteads, a mill—Eswy's a miller—we have a smithy and I'm a leather-worker."

"Are you now? That could be handy for repairs."

"Except I didn't bring as much as an awl," I said regretfully.

"We've probably got the necessary tools in a chest somewhere, but take my advice, don't mention your trade for the moment or you'll have men on at you to mend their shoes, sheaths and goodness knows what else." He laid a hand on my arm, "Concentrate on training. It could save your life and that of others, Aella."

The other men around our fire were friendly too. I soon

realised that camp life produced trust and friendship. There was lots of teasing, especially because neither Edwy nor I had beards like them. We both had moustaches after the manner of our village. I'd not asked myself why our menfolk chose to shave their chins, leaving only the upper lip whiskered. I told Edwy,

"The first thing I'm going to do is stop shaving. Anyway, there was no time to bring my razor. It'll stop them having fun at my expense."

"You're right, I'll do the same."

In a matter of days, there was a noticeable shadow along the jaw. It didn't stop the wags though, they simply teased us about the slowness of growth, which wasn't true, but I was learning fast how to reply with witticisms of my own. Our banter earned Edwy and me many friends, also on the training ground, where the wooden mock weapons could still clout hard enough to make your senses reel. On the whole, I showed considerable skill with the axe and my nimbleness saved me many a violent knock. When I suffered a setback, I never bore a grudge and would always grin and joke with my assailant. Edwy followed my example but he had more difficulty with swordsmanship and ended up with many a painful bruise. I felt sorry for him but we were learning the hard way and I knew that one day this tough work would reap its reward.

I guessed that before April was out another thirty men had joined our ranks after us, taking the number of the warband to over a hundred. Sibbald confirmed this impression.

"One hundred and forty-eight to be exact. I know, because my task is to kit everyone out. There are only a few weapons and breastplates left. We began with one hundred and sixty-five of them...so you see."

I overheard Berhtred ask how many remained and he said, "seventeen."

This elicited a snort.

"I've about had enough of this rounding up recruits. Tomorrow, your group will come with me to Hexham. We'll make up the numbers in town. Bring your weapons in case of trouble lads."

This meant that Edwy and I, along with the other six, Sibbald included, would accompany our leader into the settlement. I knew it was the biggest in the area; I'd rarely left our village but my father had told me about it. He'd lived there with my grandsires when he was young. I was excited to leave the seclusion of the forest and felt proud to set off as a recognised warrior.

TWO

HEXHAM, BERNICIA, APRIL 684 AD

UPHILL AND DOWN DALE, WE TRAMPED AND I COULD SEE why Berhtred had such muscular thighs—so his legs devoured the miles. Woe betide us if we slackened the pace, it meant a stinging cuff around the ear that set it ringing and smarting. Once was more than enough to keep a man on his toes. So, we arrived in Hexham in good time. The odours of human occupation were suffocated by a tannery on the outskirts of town. The others pulled faces and wrinkled their noses, but in my trade, I was used to the stench of those places.

"By Thunor, what *is* that foulness?" Edwy grimaced.

I laughed and showed off my knowledge,

"The hides have become pelts. Look they're tipping them into vats of dog dung and chicken droppings." I chose my words carefully, avoiding vulgarity, to lend them greater weight.

"Why would they do that?" my friend asked.

"To open the pores in the leather."

"It stinks to the sky!" Sibbald grumbled.

"I'll never wear leather again," Edwy said.

"In the end, after steeping and oiling, it comes out clean enough."

"What do they oil it with, Aella?"

I frowned, it depended on supply,

"Well, either with fish oil or animals' brains. It softens the leather and makes it supple."

"In the name of Woden," Sibbald said, "who in his right mind would be a tanner by trade?"

I laughed, and nudged him, "No tanners, and there'd be no leather; no leather, and there're no boots, clothing, shields, and armour, tents, bottles and buckets, just to name a few things."

"I suppose you're right. But the townsfolk did right to set them beyond the houses and downwind at that."

"You can't gainsay that!" Edwy chirruped.

Chuckling, we marched on into the town, where the smells were still close to overpowering as the filth had accumulated in the streets along with scavenging crows, kites and rats flapping or scurrying in a constant whirl of movement.

Ten summers past, monks had founded an abbey near the marketplace and we caught sight of an agitated group of brown-clothed brethren around a cart with a broken wheel. The burden was well covered, but the load must have been heavy and the solid wheel had ceded at its joints.

I am practical and, feeling I could help, called a halt.

"Lord Berhtred, let us aid these poor fellows!"

"Ay, help them," he said gruffly.

I gave orders and our lads hoisted the cart so that the wheel no longer touched the road surface. I picked up a rock and knocked out the oak peg passing through the axle.

Berhtred who had been looking on, leapt forward to lend a hand to lay the wheel on the ground. Without hammer and nails, nothing could be done to repair it.

"Hammer and nails!" I cried.

The fellows holding up the cart were beginning to suffer and two of the monks joined to help keep it suspended. Two minutes later, a wiry man with filthy long hair came running, a hammer in his hand. He pulled nails out of his tunic and handed them to me, too breathless to speak. A few well-placed nails strengthened the broken joints and in moments, Berhtred and I had the wheel back on its axle. I whacked the oak peg back into place and straightened up with a smile, calling,

"Set it down, lads, gently does it!"

With a groan, the cart settled under its load.

"It'll see you home, brothers, until you can get a wheelwright to change it."

"We have no money for your services, friend."

"And I would take none," I smiled.

He untied a string from around his waist, bearing a wooden cross.

"Then, take this. Our God will keep you safe."

I tried to protest that I wasn't a Christian, but he silenced me.

"Keep it with you at all times and God will protect you."

I didn't know about that, but I *did* know about amulets and their magical power. This was surely, the same thing, so I stifled my protests, turning them into thanks and wore my new charm proudly over my tunic. I watched their ox heave away the creaking cart with satisfaction and a hefty clap on the back set me arching again.

"Well done, Aella, you're a useful fellow to have around!"

I think that was the only praise I'd had so far from grumpy Berhtred, so it meant a lot to me. But that was nothing compared with what was to come inside the blade grinder's workshop. There, Berhtred spotted a likely-looking youth and signalled Edwy to seize him. This he did, but at the same time, the grinder straightened from over his work and began to shout and curse.

"You leave him be, you devil's spawn! Do you hear? That's my boy you've got there!"

"Hark!" cried Berhtred, "King's orders, he's to come to war and you'll obey your ruler!"

The man shook his fist and a vein stood out on his neck,

"The boy's only ten and five winters—unhand him, I say!"

Except me, everyone was staring at the grinder's antics. I'd noticed a greybeard in the darkened corner of the workshop behind a bench littered with tools and weapons. At least three-score summers to his wiry frame, the old man seized a knife and hurled it straight for Berhtred.

"Look out!" I yelled and raised my shield to protect our leader. With a thud, the knife embedded in the stout linden wood. I did not doubt that it would have found its target without my timely intervention. Berhtred grasped the hilt of the knife and with his massive strength freed it from deep in the shield. He examined the skilfully balanced blade, designed to fly with accuracy.

"Mmm, a handy weapon," he feigned concentration on the knife, but in one cat-like movement before any of us realised, it was slicing through the air back whence it came. Another thud, and the blade buried to the hilt in the old man's chest. His eyes widened, his mouth gurgled and a crimson flow issued from his lips as he sank to the floor.

"You've killed my grandsire!" The youth howled and struggled in Eswy's arms. A ferocious blow to the ear from Berhtred stilled him and he wailed in pain and despair.

"You!" Berhtred pointed at the grinder. "I have changed my mind. You'll come with us too and this brat will be your responsibility. One false move and I'll slay him rather than look at him, understood?"

The man nodded mutely and came to embrace his weeping son. I stepped over to the dead man and pulling the knife from his chest, wiped it on his tunic and stuck it in my belt. It was too valuable a weapon to waste. Besides, I felt that I'd earned this prize. I would practise and become as proficient as Berhtred.

Berhtred, who was now beaming at me.

"Aella, I have you to thank for two reasons: first, you saved my skin; second, you taught these ragamuffins here a lesson in how we cover each other's backs. Got that, you wastrels? If it hadn't been for Aella's alertness, it would've been *me* stretched out on yon floor!"

I felt ten feet tall and like a fully-fledged warrior—even if that was overdoing it a little. But I had initiated my shield and that was more than Edwy could boast.

We scoured the town, for Berhtred was determined to procure stronger bodies for our warband than the grinder and his son provided. He made no move until he found a giant as tall as himself. He pointed him out and said, "Aella, fetch him to me!"

My heart sank. This brute was twice my size but I refused to let my comrades sense my fear for all that my knees had turned to gelatine. I strode up to him, tapped his chest with a finger and looked him in the eye. That was even worse for me, his furious grey eyes turned to flint and his broad flat-nosed face came close to mine.

"What!" he bellowed, no more than an inch from my nose.

Luckily, my companions could see me but couldn't hear my squeaky voice, feeble with terror.

"You'd better come with me, friend," I croaked, "see that giant over there? Well, he wants you and if you don't come, he'll strike your head off."

Was that consternation on his face? I dearly hoped so. I

watched the grey eyes swivel and fix Berhtred. He stared for a long moment, then turned back to me.

"Plucky little fellow, aren't you?" He growled, slapped me on the back, something like a buffet from Berhtred, "Let's go see what he wants, then."

He linked arm under mine, just like a close companion, my feet hardly touching the ground, and we made straight for our leader.

"I brought him, Lord," I said, against all evidence to the contrary—if anyone had done the bringing, it was the giant.

They were all impressed, nonetheless, and it turned out that the man had been a former warrior in the Mercian War and was glad of a chance to fight again. Berhtred was delighted to have netted himself such a specimen.

"In the shield-wall, he'll be worth any two of you!" he trumpeted, but he beamed at me as he said it.

By mid-afternoon, we had brought our numbers to completion so that a group of two-dozen men left Hexham on the trail back to the forest. Our task had been made easier by the inclusion of three very strong men, who, once enrolled, took upon themselves the mantle of enforcers and guardians so that no thought of fleeing ever entered the head of any recruit. In any case, refusal to do the king's bidding was tantamount to treason and would have led to death or outlawry.

Among the foot-weary, I returned to camp with my heart singing. I had acquitted myself well and Berhtred, our leader, made his approval clear. Maybe, I thought, life away from the village wasn't so bad, after all. With our number complete, there would be no further forays other than to replenish the food store, rapidly diminishing with one hundred and sixty stomachs to satisfy.

Our mornings were filled with arms training—often we were lined up in two opposing shield-walls to experience the expenditure of strength required to hold the might of the enemy at bay. A few weeks of this, and I noticed that not just *my* arm muscles were bulging, but also those of Edwy. In this, he had a head start over me, from his years of humping sacks of grain and flour.

I chose to spend my afternoons some distance from my comrades where I could practise throwing my deadly knife. I used a kerchief snagged on a tree as a target and after a few sessions, I was able to rip it in half to make a smaller target. I numbered so many hits that the cloth was shredded and not much use so that I had to beg a rag from one of our comrades. This I cut into small squares and became so skilful at throwing the knife that I took it as an affront if I missed—this happened rarely, and only if I'd driven myself too hard.

Imagine my dismay when I realised I was being spied upon. At first, I wasn't sure, noting branches twitching, which might simply, in my mind, have been caused by a large bird. But one day, when I heard a cough suppressed and spotted a flash of yellow cloth as I approached, followed by a footfall running away, and I knew it wasn't my imagination.

A few days later, I noticed a fellow from another group casting envious glances at my knife thrust into my belt and he was wearing a dirty *yellow* tunic. I decided that I'd keep a wary eye on him, but he was too crafty. He sneaked up at night and coolly slid the knife from under my belt. I found it missing in the morning, which is when I sought him out to accuse him of the theft. Of course, he feigned outrage and made a scene, which ended in us pushing and shoving each other before fists flew. Then, my comrades came a-running to my aid, shouting,

"What's going on?"

"This fellow's stolen my throwing knife."

"Liar! Prove it!"

This is where I was grateful to Sibbald,

"Oh, we will right enough!" he said, tipping out the man's pack on the ground. Of course, too obvious, it wasn't there among his belongings. But Sibbald, astute as a stoat in winter, tossed the man's pallet of ferns, and blankets aside and studied the soil under it.

I knew at once and so did Sibbald, who leant over the spot where the earth had been freshly disturbed and dug into the soft ground with the point of his seax. In moments, he was brandishing my knife for all to see.

"I don't know how that got there!" the wretch said lamely and even his companions, who were spoiling for a fight with mine, sneered and hissed 'nithing'.

Sibbald marched him at seax point, with many a threat, to Berhtred to accuse him of theft.

Since this was a grave matter, I was pleased that the case was irrefutable. Also, I was Berhtred's favourite at the time. Our leader listened to the accusation and looked as if he would strangle the thief with his bare hands. When the thunder had cleared from his face, he said, "Ina," for that was his name, "there are witnesses to your theft and you know the penalty. I will have no thieving in this camp. You will forfeit ten silver pennies to be paid to Aella before the setting of the sun. You will both come here to me when the sun touches the top of yon tallest tree."

Ina blanched because ten silver pennies was a fair sum in that, the fourteenth, year of King Ecgfrith's reign. I did not doubt that the miserable thief had spent all afternoon begging around the camp for silver coins. When he came with leaden steps to join me before Berhtred's tent as the sun sank to the treetops, he glared at me as though I had injured him, not the other way around.

"Have you brought the ten pieces of silver, Ina?" Berhtred boomed.

The wretch trembled, and began to snivel,

"Nay, Lord, I could not raise the sum. I made a terrible mistake. I beg Aella to forgive me. It was a moment of weakness."

"That it was not!" I glowered at him, "I know you planned to steal my knife for many days and you sneaked up in the night when everyone was asleep to spirit it away. Not satisfied, you buried in the ground where you thought nobody would find it. What do you say to that?"

"It's true and I wronged you, but now I'm pleading with you."

"Silence!" Berhtred bellowed and glared around the small crowd that was forming to see justice dispensed. "The law is clear on this," he continued, "if the stipulated sum is not paid in the stated time, the thief must lose a hand."

Ina cringed and whimpered, "Lord, I beg of you...Aella... have mercy!"

I decided at that moment that I would pity him, only not as he meant it.

Berhtred grasped Ina by the arm. Even the strongest man in the camp couldn't have broken that grip. There was no chance of flight.

Aella, find a decent log and bring your axe. The hand is yours to take!"

I hurried away and found a sturdy fallen branch, a yard long. Next, I fetched my axe.

"A good clean blow," Edwy advised, "Don't hesitate."

He walked beside me back to Berhtred, breathing words of encouragement and condemnation of Ina. It strengthened my resolve as I tossed the log on the ground at their feet.

"No!" shrieked the wretch, his eyes wild.

"You asked for mercy, and I will give it to you."

"What!" exclaimed Berhtred, his face a mask of fury.

I smiled at him and said,

"Ina, are you keck-handed or do you use your right?"

"My right!" he screamed.

"Then I will take the left and count yourself lucky!"

At this, Berhtred roared with mirth and pinned the left arm of the villain to the ground at the elbow.

"Lower your wrist to the log or it'll go far worse for you," I cried.

As if in a bad dream, I raised the axe and brought it down with all my new-found strength. When I stepped back, I looked in horror, as if I hadn't delivered the blow, at the gushing blood and the hand with its curled fingers severed on the ground.

I always kept my blade whetted and fit to shave with, so the strike had been clean.

"Quick!" shouted Berhtred, "Fetch a brand to seal the wound!"

This was done among the screams of the victim and he lived to fight with a shield strapped to his left arm. It may not seem like it, but I had, indeed, performed an act of mercy by allowing Ina to retain his weapon hand so that he could engage in combat like a man in battle.

I avoided crossing his path whenever he was in the vicinity, so the matter of his mutilation remained a distant thought—at least for me.

THREE

BABBANBURGH, NORTHUMBRIA, MAY 684 AD

OUR SOJOURN IN THE FOREST ENDED AS BRIGHTNESS flooded the dell at the end of April ushering in stable sunny weather. The mild days brought Berhtred's decision to break up camp, load the carts and move out. My comrades had no better idea than mine as to our destination. Sibbald continued to mutter about the sea and when the first gulls and terns appeared overhead and the air freshened and bore the tang of salt, it looked as if he was right.

I had never boarded a ship in my life, but any fear of a voyage was momentarily suspended because it was to the king's stronghold we were directed. On the Northumbrian coast, standing high on a crag overlooking the restless sea, lay the imposing fortress of Babbanburgh. My father had told me how in his father's day—two lifetimes before—the king at the time, Aethelfrith had gifted the place to his wife, Queen Bebba. That's how it got its name: Bebba's burgh. I shared my knowledge with Edwy, who looked suitably impressed and in a low voice so as not to be heard by the others, said,

"Aella, do you think we'll manage to see the king?"

I looked up at the towering walls and wondered.

"We're going there, so I reckon we might catch a glimpse, but the likes of us won't be allowed too close."

That shows how wrong we can be about predicting our fates; although I still haven't met the man who can tell me what the morrow will bring. Some know what the weather will do, fishermen and the like, but that's not what I mean.

Berhtred ordered the blast of a horn to be sounded before the gate and after an exchange of shouts, the great wooden barrier swung back. We tramped inside and our carts creaked into the vast courtyard where Berhtred lined us up in serried ranks. As my wyrd would have it, I was in the middle of the front row with Edwy so that we had an unobstructed view of King Ecgfrith. The king was talking with a grey-haired man with a pleasant unfurrowed face despite his age.

"Is he pointing at me?" I whispered to Edwy because the eyes of both men seemed to be locked on me.

"I think they're staring at you," Edwy confirmed my impression.

But why? I wasn't important and much as I had wished to see the king, I hadn't wanted him to notice *me*. Their attention soon shifted and King Ecgfrith moved over to Berhtred and exchanged a few words. This was only natural, but what wasn't normal was when Berhtred turned to stare at me. What had the king said to make him do that? It was as if our leader was seeking confirmation that I was the one the king was talking about. He turned back immediately to the monarch and they continued their conversation.

At last, Ecgfrith re-joined his previous companion, who to my relief, didn't look my way. I began to relax when Berhtred's bellowing voice silenced us all.

"You have the rest of today free. What you do with it is your business, but heed me well...I want you all here at dawn on this ground lined up as you are now—king's orders. Tomorrow, we move out! Any man causing trouble in Babbanburgh will feel this!" He raised a massive fist and everyone knew what that was capable of…I didn't doubt that all the men would be on their best behaviour. I knew I would. "Dismissed!" he roared.

I was about to turn and discuss with Edwy what to do next when a familiar huge hand rested on my shoulder: Berhtred!

"Aella, the king wishes to see you in the palace, now. Come with me! You can come too, you're his friend."

Edwy looked as delighted as I looked dismayed. The king wished to see *me*, but what had I done?

"What's this about, Lord?"

"Blessed if I know, Aella, but you have done nothing to displease me. I even told the king that you saved my life."

I thought that was very kind of him but didn't know how to thank him without making a fool of myself, so followed up the steep steps to the king's hall as tongue-tied as I've ever been. Affected in this way by the enormity of meeting the king, the impact of the occasion heightened when I gazed at the writhing carvings of the doorpost. I'd never seen such skilful workmanship. Inside the palace was no less splendid, the vast space with a huge hearth in the centre, surrounded by tables. On the walls, hung coloured woven drapes with emblems. I recognised the gold and dark red bars of the royal banner—the largest of them.

As we walked, the unmistakable essence of lavender was released underfoot. The dried flowers interspersed among the fresh rushes served this purpose. To some extent, the scent compensated for the smoke in the air from the blazing fire in the centre even if most of it escaped through a hole in the middle of the roof.

The king sat on a solid oak throne raised on a dais and next to him on another importantly carved seat reclined the grey-haired man, who had stared at me outdoors.

Berhtred approached them, indicating with a hand that we should wait our turn.

"Sire, I have brought Aella, who you pointed out and his friend Edwy. They are from the same village near Hexham."

"Come!"

King Ecgfrith gestured and we stepped forward to within a yard of the monarch. There, I remembered what my grandsire had told me. When in his youth, he had knelt before King Aethelfrith, so I dropped to my knees and after a hesitation, Edwy did likewise.

The king smiled and looked at our commander,

"I see you have your men well trained, Berhtred."

Honest to a fault, he replied, "My men are well-trained, Sire, but not to kneel. This is the work of Aella's wit: as sharp as ever."

"Stand up!" the king gave me an appraising look—a very positive one, I felt. "Aella, this is Bishop Cuthbert," he indicated the man next to him. "He is my bishop of Lindisfarne."

I looked puzzled but the king was an intelligent man and read it swiftly in my face. "I see you do not know the name. It is a tidal island just off this coast. Many people call it, *Holy Island,* for it was there Cuthbert's predecessor Saint Aidan founded a monastery in my father's lifetime. I swear that Cuthbert is a saint too!"

I had about as much idea of what a saint was as I had about Lindisfarne. Feeling confused, I glanced at the bishop, perhaps for help, but he was too busy denying any such title. I still wondered what I was doing talking to the king.

I discovered why immediately. When he'd finished setting the king straight about his not being a saint—which, anyway, I later learnt, he was, Cuthbert turned to me with a pleasant smile.

"I picked you out at once from among the warriors, brother. For you were the only one bearing Our Lord's Cross on his chest. My hand strayed involuntarily to my amulet.

So that's what it's about!

I thought I should clear matters up, but he asked a question and I had to answer.

"Who baptised you? Where was it done?"

I could feel my face burning.

"Nay. I have not been baptised." I knew what it meant because my mother had told me about the new religion although she, like all our family believed in the old gods.

"A monk gave me this, did he not?" I turned to Lord Berhtred, who nodded, "Because I helped repair his broken cartwheel."

"Ah, a Good Samaritan!" The bishop spoke in riddles. "But would you not *like* to be baptised, Aella?"

I glanced furtively at the king and I could see him staring intently at me, which meant he cared about my answer.

Blessed with my fair share of wits, I quickly replied, "Ay, my Lord Bishop, I would."

"There is no time to prepare you properly, for you leave for war tomorrow and I would prefer you to go with my blessing and Our Lord's shield."

In my ignorance, I thought I already owned a shield—I'd left it with my weapons near the door.

"What about you, Edwy?" the bishop stared at him.

As we'd been inseparable as children, I feel sure that influenced his reply.

"I'll join Aella willingly."

"Sire, will you stand as godfather to these two young men."

The king laughed, "You deserve this honour, Aella, for

23

saving the life of one of my finest commanders. And you, Edwy, for choosing your friends well!" He chortled at his joke. "We shall go at once to my chapel. There you may use my piscina, Bishop Cuthbert."

We found ourselves listening to chants in a strange language, then to my embarrassment, ordered to strip naked and to enter the water. The Bishop took off his shoes, rolled up his robe, and pushed my head under the surface. When he let me up spluttering, he cupped his hand, all the time murmuring in a language unknown to me, and poured more water on my wet brow. There, with a finger, he made the sign of the Cross before turning to Edwy, who wasn't to be caught like me but took a deep breath first. He underwent the same curious ceremony. Then, we were allowed to dry ourselves and dress.

The Bishop took us to a bench and gave us a long lecture about how we must foreswear the old gods and all of the Devil's works. I understood most of this because he was a clear teacher and spoke our language well.

King Ecgfrith who had disappeared, now returned bearing gifts. Over my head, he looped a silver chain with a cross of the same metal. "Wear this hidden next to your skin, Aella, it will protect you against enemies in this and the other world." He gave the same gift to Edwy with the same admonishment. From his purse he took two gold coins: one each, "These are from Frankia and worth many pieces of silver. Be loyal to your king and spend them well. I will see you tomorrow at dawn." He held out his hand for a kiss.

"When he'd gone, Edwy said, "B-but it's a fortune!"

Before I could reply, Bishop Cuthbert said, "It is a fortune, Edwy, but your true blessing is to have the king as your godfather. Few men can boast a king as such. You must be forever worthy of this grace. Lead an unblemished existence and you shall both enjoy eternal life with the Father, the Creator of Heaven and Earth.

"My Lord Bishop—" I began but he interrupted.

"Call me *Your Grace*."

"Your Grace, I would like to know all about Christianity."

His smile was beatific, "And so you shall, from me, when you return from the campaign. Heaven knows I've tried to dissuade Ecgfrith from this folly, but he's set his course and he will not heed my advice."

This was our first inkling that Cuthbert was contrary to the king's battle plan against the Britons. In a gesture similar to the king's he held out his hand. On it, he wore a red ring. "Kiss the ring," he ordered and I did. I later found out that this was expected when greeting a bishop. We had a lot to learn about this new religion. For the moment, although I could feel the silver cross nestling against my chest, I was glad they'd let me keep my wooden amulet. At that moment, I was too confused to think straight, but I knew the gold coin was in my purse and as we walked out of the king's hall, to collect our weapons, I whispered to Edwy, "Not a word about our money or our other gift. We don't want envy spreading through the ranks. We should keep the gold for when we get home, you could use it for the mill and I'll save mine to buy more goats and skins. Father will be pleased—" *if he recovers.* Reluctantly, Edwy agreed to follow my advice.

Some of our comrades looked the worst for wear at the morning assembly. It seemed that the mewing gulls, making a din, provoked many a curse from those with aching heads. Edwy and I had consumed but two measures of ale, for, apart from the king's gold, between us we had but four silver pennies. Edwy grumbled when I prevailed on him to be thrifty, but recognised that there would be the right time to spend our unexpected wealth.

The king came down from the hall wearing his mail shirt with a sword strapped to his side.

He stood before us and in a ringing, kingly voice told us that we were to set sail for Ériu to put an end to the British mercenaries serving the Irish kings, whose depredations in Northumbria he would tolerate no longer. We all cheered raucously, owing to the state of their heads, some were more raucous than others. Ecgfrith was careful not to mention that the foe was the same Britons he had driven from their homeland of Rheged. I discovered this years later. For now, my main concern was the sea voyage. I'd never sailed in my life and now we were marching down to the shore to board the boats. Four ships were at anchor and each had twenty pairs of oars. Fifty men to a vessel meant that we had a force of two hundred for this campaign. Lord Berhtred said it was more than enough to defeat the Britons. Four ships did not seem a lot as I looked from one to another.

"You two, bring your group," Berhtred said. He knew all about raising morale. So, we collected Sibbald and the others and crewed on the king's ship, where Lord Berhtred kept us all on our toes. This voyage promised to be tough.

FOUR

THE SEA ROUTE NORTH OF SCOTLAND, MAY 684 AD

NOT HAVING VENTURED FARTHER THAN FIVE LEAGUES from my village until I came to Babbanburgh, the extent and topography of Northumbria was a mystery to me. Therefore, it was a privilege to be on board the king's ship, close to Lord Berhtred, who was often in conversation with our ruler. I feigned not to hear the words exchanged, but occasionally my ears stood up like those of a hare, as on this occasion,

"Sire, I beg you to appease my curious nature. There will be a good reason why have you chosen to take the long sea route around the Pictish lands when we could have sailed the short crossing from our western coast."

"Lord Berhtred, no doubt you are a mighty warrior, but conducting a successful campaign requires astute planning. Had we opted to march across our territory to the west, we would have given the Britons ample warning of our arrival and thus time to organise their resistance. They do not imagine we might ever sail so far north. You see, we'll swoop down upon them like a fox on the coop!"

"Sire, I know never to debate your wisdom."

I wasn't much clearer, not knowing how far north Scotland stretched, nor how wide it was. I hoped only that it was a small land so that my poor stomach should have some respite. Edwy suffered much more, hanging over the gunwales several times in the first three days and vomiting wretchedly. Nor was he alone; I'm sure that much of my queasiness depended on the sights and smells created by the numerous sufferers on board. The king and Lord Berhtred only laughed at the miserable fellows, being of sterner stuff themselves. Indeed, King Ecgfrith remarked that we were lucky to have such settled weather for the voyage. I dread to think what the northern passage must be like in a gale.

On one occasion, Berhtred told Edwy, sitting on a coiled rope trying to recover from his latest bout of seasickness, "Don't worry, my friend, soon we'll enter the Irish Sea and it won't be long till we're camping on dry land."

Never were words so welcome to my ears. Of course, he failed to mention the diabolical currents, which swayed and rocked our ships far more than the North Sea.

One misty morning, the sight of the shrouded mainland brought a cheer from us weary seafarers and within an hour, we were wading ashore with heavy packs on our backs, struggling against the waves to keep a footing and to save them from the water.

Rarely have I blessed the ground under me as much as that night, sitting quaffing ale with my comrades by a fire. The king had sensibly deployed lookouts to guard our camp. He also sent out spies to determine the whereabouts of the British mercenaries. Well aware of the cunning of the Britons, he meant to be the one to deliver a surprise.

The next day at mid-morning, one of the scouts arrived on the back of a mule he had stolen.

"Lord Berhtred, I must see the King, I know where the Britons have their base."

"Tell me, man, I'll inform King Ecgfrith." He pressed a coin into the fellow's hand. "Well done. Now, where are they lurking?"

"Down the coast, Lord. Those that have not sailed across to our lands are settled in a small town. Forgive me, I cannot pronounce the name, but it is three leagues away. The Britons have ships in the harbour."

"You will lead us there! I shall inform the King."

At these words, I began to make ready, strapping on my leather breastplate and greaves.

"Hey! What are you doing?" Edwy had seen my preparations.

"Readying myself for war—"

But my explanation was cut short by the bellow of Berhtred, whose orders to the men I had anticipated.

Alert for the treachery of the foe, the king deployed guards to head, flank and tail our column. Berhtred ordered us to march in silence so that only the tramping of our feet could be heard, and not much at that, on the beaten earth track.

Since this was to be a surprise attack there was no question of setting a shield-wall. This would be a revenge raid, such as the ones the Britons adopted for our coastal settlements or isolated farmsteads.

"Spare none of the men, take the women and children as slaves and seize whatever valuables you can lay your hands on." The king's orders were pitiless.

This was like an invitation to a feast for the men so that the command to charge into the town was met by a fleet-footed response as if we hadn't just completed a march of three leagues. To the accompanying commotion of animals, the screams of women, the wounded and the clash of weapons, it seemed like the world was coming to an end. "This way!" Berhtred tugged me and called Edwy. He was heading for a large wooden building.

"The church," he said, "Rich pickings there—gold and silver!"

He was first through the door and straight down the nave to seize the silver candlesticks and cross. Edwy had followed him but I held back, I do not know why. Instinct made me look around the gloomy rear of the building to see a man lurking in the shadows. I went towards him, swinging my axe. I could smell his fear and in a low voice, he begged for his life. Even in this dim light, I distinguished his pallor and the beads of sweat on his countenance. His face was gentle and shaven but contorted by terror. Then, something inexplicable happened.

There was no time for conversation, so I bundled him through a door, mindful of our orders to kill all the men. Why I didn't obey, there and then, still mystifies me. Without the slightest doubt, if Berhtred had found him, he would have slit the fellow's throat on the spot. As it was, I had pushed him into the bell tower where a rope hung forlornly in the middle of the space.

I put a finger to my lips.

"Not a sound or they'll kill you," I whispered.

"Bless you, my son. God will reward you for saving his priest."

I gazed at him open-mouthed. I had no idea of who he was or his role; I simply hadn't wanted to slaughter an unarmed man. I hurried out of the tower, closed the door, to come face to face with Berhtred.

"What's in there, Aella?"

"Nothing," I tried to sound disappointed, "it's just a bell tower. There are only the bell rope and cobwebs."

"Never mind, you take this," he thrust a candlestick at my chest, "it's silver and it'll melt down nicely. Come on, let's join the others!"

It didn't occur to him to question my word and maybe he mistook my sigh of relief as a reaction to his gift.

We left the church to the sight of flames blazing from the homes and bodies scattered in the street. Women wailed and men shouted, not least our king, who lacked Berhtred's booming authority, and therefore whose attempts to restore discipline were having little effect. Our commander took over, his swinging fist more persuasive than his voice. Soon, we were ready to move out, but not before King Ecgfrith sent a group of men to the harbour to set fire to the anchored ships. As dusk enfolded the land, the blazing houses and vessels cast a ruddy glow over the few pallid faces not already spattered with gore.

The prisoners, women and children, were herded the three leagues back to the encampment where we had left several men to guard the tents and our ships. Before cresting the rise, I stared back at the devastation. The red fires on land and sea under billowing smoke recited a crackling tale of vengeance to anyone unfortunate enough to hear it. One man, for sure, would do so: the one I had spared. Whether the slaughtered men were Britons or Irish, I could not say. The presence of the ships seemed to suggest that our spy had been right: that this had been a British settlement preparing to attack our homeland. Those raiders would never arrive to plunder, rape and rob.

Wearily, we arrived at our encampment, bound the prisoners' hands and legs and placed them in a hollow with guards around them. Before I lay by the fire, too weary to drink, I put the candlestick into a linen bag next to my other possessions. Sibbald watched me and muttered,

"The next place we attack, I'm going straight for the church."

Curled up in my blanket, I thought back over the day's events. I hadn't killed a single enemy; instead, I had saved one. This thought disturbed me. Why had I done it? What strange impulse had made me save the priest—a man unknown to me? Many troubled explanations came to mind—not least, I wondered whether it been my new God that had guided me unknowingly into sparing his servant? Was that possible? No, I dismissed the idea. After all, I had become a Christian merely to ingratiate myself with the king. Ay, that was plain enough—I liked to be clear on my motives, but I couldn't find a single one for letting the priest live. The inexplicable perturbed me, but I was too weary to stay awake fretting.

Our warband raided four more settlements and although I killed my share of enemies, I took no part in the plundering of the churches. I saw no harm in taking a gold armlet from a slain red-haired foe, his face daubed with blue paint, but steered well clear of places of worship. The fact is, I wasn't doing avoiding them consciously because if I thought about it rationally, the pickings were easy, and I could not explain why I refrained, nor, for the moment, was I bothered by my reticence. Sibbald boasted about his silver cross and ascribed my sour expression to jealousy, which it was not. I felt that something was wrong and longed for my simple life as a leather-worker.

It came as a relief when King Ecgfrith deemed the reprisals sufficient and ordered us to the ships. Berhtred confirmed that we would be taking the direct route across the Irish Sea. This would be a much shorter voyage and with the benefit of the following wind. Edwy was just as sick as before and when we finally returned ashore, he whispered that he'd never set foot in a ship again.

"Maybe we won't have to," I reassured him, "as we both have enough money now, gathered one way or another, to make a great success of our trades back home."

The thought cheered us, but then neither of us had any idea of what the king was mulling over.

FIVE

LINDISFARNE AUGUST 684 AD

ANY THOUGHTS ABOUT GOING HOME THAT EDWY AND I nurtured were nipped in the bud when I asked Lord Berhtred.

"The king has ordered me not to disband our force. There's no chance of your returning to your village Aella, at least, not until next summer is over. King Ecgfrith is waiting for next spring and then we move again. The weather should be better where we're headed."

"Not Ériu again," I groaned.

He grinned, "No, not Ériu!" but would say no more.

This meant we had to stay in Babbanburgh and, apart from getting my candlestick melted down into small ingots, there was little for me to do except weapon practice. So, I went to Berhtred and asked if I could have leave to visit Bishop Cuthbert. He gave me a quizzical look,

"Don't tell me you're becoming a Christian, after all!"

"Would that be so bad?"

"Just don't let it make you soft. I prefer my warriors to be as tough as your old leather!"

I reassured him that I only wanted to find out more about

the religion I'd accepted and he permitted me, saying that he'd send Edwy to fetch me if my presence was needed.

I approached the shore.

"Hey! Where d'ye think yer goin'?"

A fisherman sitting on a bollard called to me as I reached the pathway to the island. The weather-beaten face crinkled into a broken-toothed smile.

"Can't ye tell yon tide's comin' in? If ye wants to be crossin' to Lindisfarena, ye'd best be waitin' for the ebb tide."

"And when will that be, friend?"

"I can see yer a landlubber! Ye just come an' wait here by me an' I'll tell yer when it's safe to cross. There's many a pilgrim got himself into trouble wi' yon tide rip. It's a league across from here to yonder, ye know."

I thanked him for the information and watched him mend his net, learning that his favourite time for fishing was the last hour before darkness fell.

At last, gazing out to sea, he said, "It's on the turn, now."

I didn't know what he meant.

"The *tide*, it's on the turn. You can cross now and it'll be safe until mid-afternoon. Ye just follow the retreating waves if ye can't wait any longer."

I made my way slowly across the sand and mudflats until, after more than an hour, I reckon, I struggled onto the island amid its dunes, scattering piping, protesting oystercatchers as I plodded ashore. From the top of a dune, I looked back at the mainland and fancied it was nearer than the three miles the fisherman had said, although my legs told me otherwise. The place seemed large from where I was standing but the net-mender had said the isle was three miles from east to west and half as long from north to south.

I found a track and followed it towards what I supposed would be the centre of the island and soon came to the wooden enclosure of the monastery. At the gate, I asked a monk for Bishop Cuthbert, but he took me by the arm and led me away from the entry and pointed to a path.

"You'll find the bishop in the church. Just follow the track that way. You can't go wrong." He scurried back to his post. I wondered if I would be the only person to seek something of the fellow that day—his seemed a very boring job.

Less than four hundred yards down the trail and I was gazing at a building made of hewn oak, in those days its roof made of reeds. When I returned years later, it was covered in lead. Bishop Cuthbert was inside the church deep in prayer. Loth to disturb him, I sat on one of the sturdy wooden benches behind him. He heard the movement, I'm sure, because not long after, he murmured, "Amen," made the sign of the cross and turned to stare towards me. On seeing me, he rose quickly and clasped his head in his hands,

"Oh, my head, I mustn't jump up like that!"

I wondered if his health was as good as it might be.

He beamed at me, "It *is* you, Aella! Back from the war. Tell me, are you well?"

"Your Grace, I thank you, very well. I have come in search of learning. You once said you would teach me about the faith upon my return. Well, I am back," I ended lamely.

He grinned and took my hand, "So it shall be," he said, "but not here in God's house. Come, it'll be better done in His wide world. I know just the place!"

The bishop led me away from the church and farther still from the monastery towards the sound of crashing waves.

"There's a lovely little cove down here, Aella, I come here whenever I want to contemplate. I was used to the life of a hermit, you know?"

I did not. There was so much I wanted to learn about him

and I told him so as we sat on the springy turf among the purple sea thrift and tiny yellow tormentil.

"You wish to know about me, Aella? Surely, Our Lord Jesus would be a more appropriate subject. I am but a poor wretch."

"But one, Your Grace, who has stayed in my thoughts since the day we met."

"Well, God moves in mysterious ways, Aella, so I shall do your bidding. Although Heaven knows, I do not like talking about myself." Bishop Cuthbert took a deep breath and began,

"Now, *Kenwith*, I like speaking about *her!*"

"Kenwith?" I wondered who the woman was and what she meant to him.

As if reading my mind, he said, "She was my foster-mother. I did not know my true parents, so she was a mother to me. Did you know, I was a warrior, like you, Aella.? My foster-father had me trained in arms, as a young man and I fought in a battle."

I swear he shuddered.

"But that all changed when I was on guard duty one night and had a vision."

There was something strange and rapt in his expression that made me think he was reliving the experience.

"I did not know it then, but that night, at that precise moment, the blessed saint, Aidan, died—he who founded the monastery here, Aella. I saw a peculiar light in the starry sky and it carried to Heaven a soul." He seized my arm, "It was the soul of Aidan and the brilliance must have been an angel. I made up my mind on the instant, although I could not abandon my post. Within days I had taken my leave of my comrades and marched through Lauderdale to the new monastery of Melrose. I wished to be admitted as a novice. I said as much at the gate, where by God's grace, Prior Boisil was stationed."

Cuthbert paused with a faraway look in his eyes, then said, "He was a disciple of the same Aidan and upon seeing me and hearing my request, he uttered, *Behold, the servant of the Lord!* You see, Aella, he understood and told me that I would rise to a high degree in the Church. He *knew,* just like I know with *you.*"

"With *me?*" I protested—I, who had no intention of becoming a churchman.

Cuthbert, who was endowed with extraordinary shrewdness, smiled,

"I do not mean that you will be a bishop or even a priest, Aella, but I assure you, God has chosen you for his work. I know this!"

I wondered what he meant, but letting the matter be, breathed deeply and pressed him to continue his life story.

"Once accepted into the priory at Melrose, the saintly Boisil befriended me and taught me the sacred scriptures of which, I, like you, was ignorant. I became his close companion and together we went on a mission preaching from village to village and, undoubtedly, Boisil's knowledge of curative herbs enhanced his reputation, for he treated the sick with much success. The prior could foretell the future, Aella, prophecy is a gift of God. The holy man predicted the plague that would sweep the land and claim his body. He also foretold that I, too, would succumb but that God would spare me." Cuthbert stared at me as if to test my stance on the matter. In a measured voice, he said, "All this came about. When he died, I became Prior of Melrose according to his divination. And yet, I fear the life of settled administration is not for me. You do not know this, but my present position was thrust upon me against my will. It went like this: at Melrose, I continued preaching in the countryside and left my duties to be fulfilled by a good man: my vice-Prior. My long absences were ascribed, thankfully, to my proselytising—"

"What's that?"

"It means bringing men into Christ's fold."

"Ah!"

He smiled and went on,

"Anyway, I made an oratory at a place in the north called Dull, with a stone cross and a cell for me to contemplate..." he raised a hand and pointed around, "...look around you, my friend, gaze upon the beauty of God's Creation, does a man not need time to ponder it?"

I picked a five-petalled tormentil and handed the splendid tiny yellow flower to him, saying,

"Is this not just as perfect as the restless sea or the sun in the sky?"

He opened his eyes wide, leant over me and, to my surprise, planted a kiss on my cheek.

"That is the most beautiful thing I have heard, Aella, in many a long day. I am not wrong. God *has* chosen you."

"Ay, but what for?" I muttered.

"He will show you your path in His good time, my friend."

"Now, what was I saying?" Despite his strong intellect, he was distracted and I helped him,

"You were telling me about Melrose Priory."

"Ah yes, but I retired from there and went to live on a small isle over yonder." He pointed behind us.

"Do you mean another island near here?"

"Ay, in a cave."

I was aghast, "But weren't you lonely and cold?"

"Lonely? Never, not with God's presence."

I gasped. This man was truly different from any I had known.

"And cold? Ay, of course. But Our Lord suffered agonies

for us on the Cross. Do you know ought of his five wounds, Aella?"

I admitted what little I knew was from my foster-mother's garbled accounts, so he patiently recounted the Easter story of Jesus Christ. When he'd finished, I was suitably moved and he flung a hand round my shoulders.

"Be not sorrowful, for it is a tale of joy—how Our Lord rose on the third day for our redemption!"

"I want you to tell me more about this, Your Grace, but first, you must finish your story."

He gave me the hardest possible look to interpret. At first, I thought it was withering or angry, but later, I came to believe it was a mixture of embarrassment and modesty. Luckily, he continued,

"There's not much more to tell. I have fifty winters weighing on me and think that soon God will call me to Him. People came to seek my counsel on the island, for no man may completely shut himself off from the world. In my absence from Melrose, oddly, my reputation for sanctity grew. One day, King Ecgfrith and a group of people came to persuade me to take up the bishopric of Hexham. But I refused. I cared too deeply for the contemplative life. In the end, I agreed to exchange bishoprics with the obliging Bishop Eata, who was bishop here on Lindisfarena. It suits me better to be near the sea, Aella."

"I understand."

"And now you and I are here, brother. We will come every day unless it rains. I will instruct you in the sacred scriptures, as Boisil, of blessed memory, taught me." And so, he did and we became the firmest friends. To tell the truth, he grew into a hero for me—not every paragon needs to wield a weapon. Cuthbert was the strongest man I ever met, stronger even than Berhtred—but not physically, in another way.

Before this first day's conversation was brought to an end, I had the pressing matter of the occurrence in Ériu to raise. I recounted the episode of how I had unwittingly spared the priest.

I could see the thunder on his brow when he learnt of the sacking of the churches.

"God will surely punish Ecgfrith for this sacrilege," he said, eyes full of sorrow. "But, Aella, every time you open your mouth, the conviction grows in me that God has chosen you."

Again! This insistence unnerved me.

"I must explain to you the concept of god in three persons."

When he had finished, he stared hard at me,

"Now do you understand, Aella?"

"I-I think so. You are saying that the Holy Spirit intervened to move me to spare the life of that priest."

"You are a good student: a swift learner."

I think that, rather, he was a gifted teacher. Even so, I felt compelled to declare:

"But I felt no sign that the Holy Spirit was working within me."

He laughed and patiently explained how much effort was needed to achieve a state of grace. Promising to help me attain it by teaching me how to pray and the benefits that would accrue, he brought this first session to an end. As we walked towards the monastery, I had a profound sense of change in my life. Mostly, I recognised that I had found a hero and the good fortune to be befriended by such a man. Even so, I could not begin to suspect that day, just how influential Bishop Cuthbert would be in my life. Meanwhile, I spent the whole of winter in the monastery, learnt to pray and follow the rhythms of monastic life. I spent my first Christmas there and learn about the Babe of Bethlehem.

SIX

NECHTANSMERE, MAY 20, 685 AD

THE NEW YEAR BROUGHT MOUNTING TENSION BETWEEN Bishop Cuthbert and King Ecgfrith. The king was a headstrong character and after fifteen years on the throne, very confident and assertive of his rights. To the north of his kingdom lived a savage race of tribesmen known as the Picts. The Northern Picts were rebellious tribesmen, who Ecgfrith, with the aid of the Southern Picts had defeated some years before at the Battle of Two Rivers. All this, I learnt from my friend, Cuthbert. He also told me that the king was exasperated by sieges of his northerly outposts. The latest, now three years ago, had gone unpunished.

"Aella, I believe I'm losing my powers of rhetoric," Cuthbert said, following this utterance with a heavy sigh.

"What is the matter, Your Grace?"

"My eloquence has deserted me when I need it most. In vain, despite all my prayers, I cannot convince Ecgfrith to forgo his scheme to invade the Picts. It is a folly that will cost him and his people their lives."

Remembering what Cuthbert had told me about Boisil's

gift of prophecy and suspecting his acolyte to have the same endowment, I asked him outright.

"My dearest friend, have you had such a vision?"

He smiled with a world-weariness that made me shiver,

"Not a vision, Aella, but an intuition. God nudges my thoughts in the direction He wishes them to take, and this happens when I am in quiet contemplation. Ecgfrith's stubbornness borders on arrogance and he will be punished for his pride and his wickedness against the churches in Ériu. Become a monk, my friend, so that you may avoid the slaughter and at the same time do God's work."

When I told him I'd think about it, his sorrowful eyes made it clear he knew I would not. With hindsight, I wish I had taken his advice, but every man has his wyrd and mine was to follow King Ecgfrith to the north.

As I recall, when we sailed around the northern lands to surprise the Britons the year before, I had wondered how far those lands stretched. Sufferers from sea-sickness, like Edwy, imagine a voyage to be interminable and, indeed, it seemed from our ship that the coast was never-ending. And yet, the vastness and inhospitable nature of that terrain surprised me.

At the end of April, Lord Berhtred sent Edwy to fetch me back to Babbanburgh. My departure from Lindisfarena was tinged by sadness because I had enjoyed my time there and learnt so much. I now considered myself a Christian and sought advice in prayer and I could not depart without taking leave of my mentor. Bishop Cuthbert had a special place in his heart for me, too, and loved me as a brother.

"Remember," he told me as I said my farewells, "never fail to pray, even in the darkest moments, Aella." And that was it. He said no more and I traipsed after Edwy to begin another stage in my life.

The good sense of waiting for the mild weather of May

became ever more apparent as we marched north. The farther in that direction we plodded, the more the lower grey skies seemed to oppress us; the stronger, too, grew the wind, and the rain we'd hoped to evade lashed and soaked us. But as the endless days of plodding through the wild, breathtaking scenery passed, so the weather improved and a settled dry spell accompanied us into the rugged land of the Northern Picts.

This was an area flanked to our west by high mountains, whereas we tramped through acres of black soil, gravel and marshes. It was a landscape of hummocks, terraces, ridges and hollows. The terrain favoured the foe, whose knowledge of the treacherous ground proved invaluable. Hitherto, we had seen neither hair nor hide of the Picts; and yet, the sensation we all had was of eyes following our every move. So adept were the savages at blending with the landscape that our scouts either saw nothing or died with their throats slit.

One morning, near a place with a lake that they later celebrated as Dun Nechtain in their language and we called *Nechtansmere* we came upon them lined up waiting for our advance. We formed at once into a formidable shield-wall and marched on steadily, beating menacingly on our shields with our seax hilts, confident of victory.

At first, we joined the enemy and with our superior practice at shield-walls were not surprised when they broke and retreated. Foolishly believing that we had all but won the day, we pressed after them to carry out the slaughter. But it was a trap. Lured into a defile among those inaccessible mountains, the Picts fell upon us from the heights in unexpected numbers. Now, it was our turn to break ranks and thus began the sorry rout.

We were pushed back towards the lake and running for our lives, I watched in horror as Edwy, two paces in front of me collapsed, flung forward by a black-fletched arrow between his shoulder blades. At a glance, I knew there was nothing I could do to save him. I think the arrowhead must have pierced his heart.

I pressed on and paradoxically it was the land that had betrayed us that saved me—either that or God did not want me standing in awe by his throne just yet. My comrades fell around me to arrows or spears in the back. There was no time to watch one's step and suddenly I lost the ground under my feet and went down into what they call a kettle hole. I was lucky that it was not full of water as it would surely have been during the winter. Instead, my quick wits told me how fortunate I had been or that my guardian angel had directed my steps. In a flash, I seized the chance of salvation. The cavity was narrow and reaching up, I could pull tufts of heather and other vegetation over it to conceal my presence. Now, I would have to be unlucky and have an enemy place his foot right above me. In that case, I would be the victim of a spear thrust spitting me like a helpless boar fallen into a woodland pit.

I heard the thunder of feet overhead and cringed into the gravelly and sandy soil that promised to save me. When, finally, the noise of pursuit had died away and I could hear only the gurgling of a nearby burn and the call of the curlew, I had to make a crucial decision. Should I move and expose myself to hostile eyes and end my days like poor Edwy in this forlorn place? The thought of my friend's demise brought tears that I angrily fought back. Why had Ecgfrith not listened to Bishop Cuthbert? The slaughter had been terrible and I felt sure the king was among the fallen—and he a man of but forty winters. The fifteen years of his reign had not been peaceful but marked by constant warfare, which on the whole he had won, leading him to exact ever more tribute.

I decided to wait for nightfall and to follow the stars to the south. I was sure it was the only way to return home unscathed. As I leant back in my pit, I reflected on the folly of our king's decision. How could he have believed that this people, the Picts, as wild and fierce as the land they inhabited could be subjugated and forced to pay tribute to him? Two hundred comrades had paid a high price for his arrogance. Not even the strong sinews of a mighty warrior like Berhtred could resist the speed and power of a barbed arrow. I also thought of the prophetic wisdom of my teacher, Cuthbert. Only later did I find out that he had travelled to Carlisle to visit the Queen. His second sight had caused him to cry out Ecgfrith's death at the moment that the king succumbed. I wondered as I shivered in the damp hole in the ground whether I would see the bishop again. If I succeeded in travelling back to Northumbria, I had no intention of presenting myself in Babbanburgh, although I had reason to call in at the monastery in Lindisfarena. First of all, I had no idea who would take the throne, although I suspected it might be Oswiu's other son, Aldfrith. Cuthbert had spoken to me about this learned prince who was now most likely in spiritual retreat on the holy island of Iona, where Saint Columba had built a refuge.

Even if Aldfrith proved to be a good and wise king, I'd had enough of following the orders of a ruler. I wished to return to the bosom of my family and take up my peaceful craft once more. I had so much still to learn and longed to see my parents after more than two years away. I didn't know whether my father was alive since I'd left him on his sickbed. If he had passed, all the more reason to return and care for my mother. This determination sustained me long enough to travel by night, aided by the area being rich in fresh drinking water. Even an inexpert fisherman such as I could hardly fail to profit from the abundance of fish. For fear of lighting a fire, assuming I could have done so in the damp surroundings, and risking attracting unwanted attention, I gutted my catch and ate the raw flesh.

Marching alone at night sometimes my thoughts went to dark places. I remembered Cuthbert's words in my moments of despair and would stop to pray for the well-being of my family. Increasingly, I decided that in the terrible case of finding both my parents had died, I would take monastic vows at Lindisfarne.

SEVEN

RIDING VILLAGE, NORTHUMBRIA, JUNE 685 AD

I was disappointed to learn that Bishop Cuthbert was not on Lindisfarena, but had gone to the west. I'd hoped to greet my friend and share the tale of my adventures. But that was one reason for my visit to the island before hurrying to my home village. The other was to recover my pack, which I had not taken on the campaign. It contained my silver ingots and the gold coin King Ecgfrith had given me. I knew it would be safe there, but I suppose it was only natural to experience relief on finding it intact and undisturbed.

With nothing else to detain me at the monastery, I decided to cross the mudflats and head for home at once. One of the brothers, who knew of my close friendship with the bishop enquired about my village in case Cuthbert wished to know my whereabouts on his return. I explained carefully that it was called Riding and lay five miles east of Hexham on the south bank of the great River Tyne and the Roman road to Corbridge.

I crossed the bridge over the Marsh Burn and a wave of sadness swept over me as I gazed farther downstream at the

Riding watermill. I would never more greet Edwy there and bask in his cheerful sunny smile. Turning quickly away, I pursued the track to our home, my heart in my mouth for fear of what I might find.

"Aella! Oh, my son!"

My mother saw me before I spotted her and came running out of the house to embrace me fit to break my back.

"Oh, how you've filled out—you're quite the warrior!"

There was no disputing that I'd changed, but more than just physically. I covered her in kisses and breathed in her ear.

"Father?"

"Come!" she cried gaily and my heart leapt. She took my hand and almost skipped towards the workshop.

So, he's alive, thank God!

My mother, always eager to play a prank, made me wait outside the door, calling,

"Oswin! There's a man come to see you! Out here with you!"

Still clutching a beveller stamp, he emerged blinking, trying to focus on his visitor. His face creased like one of his discarded offcuts of leather into the familiar smile.

"Father! I'm glad to see you well!"

"Ay, thanks to that Lord Berhtred of yours. How is he?"

"Lost! He fought alongside our king and Edwy. As far as I know, I'm the only one who came back alive."

"Oh, not Edwy!" mother cried. Tears filled her eyes. I remember him as a corn-haired scamp with skinned knees, always getting up to mischief. Oh, his poor mother!"

"He was my best friend."

Apart from Cuthbert.

We went indoors and I could not wait to surprise the old man.

"Hold out your hand, father." I stared at the calloused

palm and placed the gold coin onto it. Before he could say anything, I said, "Now we can buy all the materials we need for the workshop."

"B-but this is a fortune! How did you come by it, Aella?"

"King Ecgfrith gave it to me. He was my godfather."

My mother gasped and my father looked confused. She spoke first.

"You have become a Christian! You have been baptised!"

I had to explain what all this meant to my father, who still worshipped the old gods, especially Thunor, whom he saw as a craftsman just like himself, although I wasn't sure that Thunor used his hammer for creative purposes!

I talked for long hours about Cuthbert and my miraculous escape from the Picts. I became angry with him at that point because he refused to see my survival as divine intervention.

"You got lucky, lad. You fell in a hole and had the wit to cover yourself. And if you must put it down to something else, why, it could have been the breath of Woden that blew you into the pit!"

I was too relieved and happy to see him fit and well to argue. But I recognised that my mother would be easier to convert. She was halfway there out of curiosity.

There's nowhere as comfortable as your own bed and I slept soundly that night, comforted by finding my parents hale, and in mother's case, hearty. I woke with the thought of Edwy's family obsessing me. It was my duty to visit them and there was something I desperately needed to do. After the best breakfast I'd eaten in an age, of hot oatcake and a fried egg, I set off with my pack to seek out Edwy's parents.

Walking along the trail running alongside the March Burn, I saw a figure outside the mill, adjusting the race of the undershot flow. He straightened up, turned around and waved with a cheery grin. Edwy!

What the Devil! How can this be?

I had left him dead in the Pictish bog-land and here he was waving at me. Goosepimples rose and prickled along my arms. Was this the ghost of my best friend striding to greet me? When he drew near, I smiled, an unsuitable foolish embarrassed expression on my face as I realised who it was. I had forgotten about Nerian, Edwy's younger brother, grown two handspans in my absence. The work once performed by Edwy and now by him had broadened his shoulders and added muscles to the previous boyish frame.

"Aella! Welcome back, but what of Edwy...?"

His words trailed away as he interpreted the look clouding my countenance.

"Taken like the rest of my comrades and the King himself. We walked into a trap. I escaped by a hair's breadth. I'm deeply sorry, Nerian."

"Come indoors, Aella. I know my parents would wish to hear what happened to my brother from your mouth."

Stearc, Edwy's father, was older than mine but looked younger despite his baldness and paunch. I put it down to his ruddy cheeks and the laughter lines around his eyes: not that there was much to be cheerful about today.

"Aella! Welcome young fellow! What news of Edwy?"

I cast a fearful glance towards his skinny, grey-haired wife, Cwen, who was kneading dough to make her delicious bread in the wood-burning oven Edwy had built just outside the door.

From this subtle reaction, he feared the worst at once.

"How did it happen?"

"An arrow in the back as we were fleeing. Mercifully, he died at once. The Picts lured us into a trap, Stearc, and I've asked myself countless times what we were doing up there in their lands. You see, the likes of us do the king's bidding. He was a good king but his fight was not our struggle and..." here my voice broke and Cwen sobbed and slammed the dough on the table with all her might. "...it cost Edwy and King Ecgfrith, too, their lives." Somehow, I forced out these last words.

They invited me to sit and I did so willingly; we remained quiet for a while. Nerian poured me an ale and we drank in companionable silence. At last, I said, "I think you should know that Edwy and I converted to Christianity and that King Ecgfrith was your son's godfather. He gave us presents when we were baptised and Edwy meant to bring you his gold piece for the mill...but alas, I know not what became of it."

It's probably in the purse of some filthy Pict.

"Instead," I rummaged in my pack, pulled out one ingot after another until five of my ten bars graced the table, "it is my wish that you accept this silver. We won it in a battle against the Britons," it was a satisfactory half-truth under the circumstances. "Edwy planned to use the gold to expand your business, Stearc. The silver will serve the same purpose.

"Ay, that it will. I bless you for it, Aella. Drink another ale! And you, woman, whilst he does, get yon bread in the oven so that the lad can take a fresh loaf home."

Very soon, the delicious smell of freshly baked bread wafted through the door, making my mouth water.

"Tell us what it's like to be a warrior, Aella," Nerian pressed me, his earnest pale blue eyes, so similar to Edwy's pleaded with me.

By the time I'd finished my account of my military experiences, the eager youth of ten and six winters had extracted a promise that he could come to my house every afternoon. When his day's toil at the mill ended, he planned to learn armed combat from me. Why he might think it useful in his future life as a miller, I had no notion. His resemblance to Edwy meant I could deny him nothing and his secondary idea, to discover everything about Christianity pleased me. We had

no church or priest in Riding but a scheme for carrying on
Cuthbert's work was beginning to form in my mind.

I kissed the tearful Cwen, her sorrow tugging at my
heartstrings, clapped Nerian on the back and clasped his
father's hand before bearing my prized loaf home to my
mother, who would make grateful use of it. Stearc also pressed
me to accept a bagful of freshly ground flour, joking,

"If your mother knows not what to do with it, you could try
your hand at bread-making, Aella."

We laughed, but my chortle was as hollow as his. I was
reliving the moment when my friend had pitched over with an
arrow in his back before my horrified gaze.

The long summer passed almost in a dream after what I
had experienced. Country life is rich and rewarding if a man
applies himself. In a matter of days, I had dug out a vegetable
garden and planted seedlings obtained from the market in the
neighbouring village of Broomhaugh. There, I found a trader, a
breeder, willing to exchange my coin for a cow that had
produced her first calf. The animal would thrive and supply us
with milk. I led it home on a rope, the tender plants carefully
placed in a box clutched close to my chest. I managed these
small occupations at the same time as learning my craft as a
leather-worker by watching father's techniques as he worked.
The most important one I learnt in those early days was when
he silently glued cord to a board and tooled the leather over it.
This produced a wonderful effect on goatskin leather. I stored
it away like a treasure in the coffers of my memory, never
suspecting what use I'd make of it in years to come.

Meanwhile, an idea was nagging at the back of my mind
and having the wherewithal to pay for its attainment, I set off
one morning for Hexham. My destination was the new abbey
where I hoped to find what I sought. I felt sure that I would
because the building was made of stone and as I found out later

that same day, the construction material came from Roman ruins close to Hexham.

I found a monk, who informed me his name was Brother Tolan, prepared to guide me around the abbey for a silver coin *'for candles, brother.'* He explained that the crypt was a plain structure of four chambers, where the monks exhibited the relics which were a feature of the church. It consisted of a chapel with an ante-chapel at the west end, two side passages with enlarged vestibules and three stairways. The chapel and ante-chapel, Tolan said were barrel-vaulted and explained how the masons' skill held the place together. I was fascinated to learn that all the stones used were of Roman workmanship.

Tolan beamed at me, pleased that he had demonstrated all his knowledge with a measure of pride in the abbey that was his home and the generous mother of his learning. I had been patient and waited to gain his confidence but now the time was right to ask.

"Brother Tolan, I need the services of a skilled mason. Once I had told him the reason, he was keen to oblige."

"Come this way Master Aella," thus he called me after discovering of my trade.

Without him as a guide, I'm sure I would not have located the masons chipping away at stone in a workshop hidden behind the sacred edifice.

"This is Master Aella," said Brother Tolan, "he is a leather-worker and prepared to pay well for your services," he told Master Almund, who was in charge of the five of his team sculpting yellow-grey sandstone blocks to create angels, devils, inscribed stones and whatever stonework served for the abbey.

"What is it you want of me, Master Aella?"

I took out the silver ingot that I had brought for the purpose and laid it on the stone he'd been working in front of the mason's avid eyes.

"That will have to suffice to procure me a fine standing cross, taller than a man. It need not be too elaborate. What I need is an inscription to the memory of Edwy Stearcsson who died for his king. It should also have a Christian image, let's say Our Lord's birth or His death, whichever you prefer."

"I can do that for you if yon's mine," he nodded at the ingot, "and I'll carve you a fine border around the work, too."

"When will it be ready?"

"You'll pay for an ox and cart to haul it away?"

"Of course."

"Let's say, what, with all the work we have at the moment, the end of next month."

I picked up the ingot, and he looked anguished. But I handed it to Brother Tolan.

"You will give this to Master Almund only when my cross is finished. Will you do this for me, Brother?"

"Ay, right willingly. I'll come to check on your progress from time to time," said the benign monk.

I spat on my palm and clasped that of the mason and the pact was sealed.

Almund was a man of his word and oversaw the loading of the cart to make sure no damage would occur to his fine workmanship. I travelled backwards with my legs dangling over the back of the waggon. It was a hateful bumpy journey on the rutted roads but after several hours we arrived at Riding. We plodded through the village past the smithy to the place I had chosen for this wayside cross—where the road forked, one track leading to Slaley and the other to Corbridge. We gathered a group of villagers who helped erect the heavy stone on its huge plinth right between the tracks, facing the settlement.

In a scroll-enclosed panel was a scene portraying the Nativity while in another beneath, written in Latin I read *In*

Memoriam and other foreign words before the strange combination of letters ***DCCCLXV***—of the folks there, thanks to Cuthbert's teachings, I was the only one who knew it was the date of this year, 865 AD. The other carved words I and everyone else present could read were: ***Edwy Stearcsson*** and ***Egfridus Rex***. Translating the king's name was all very well, but I was glad Master Almund had refrained from trying to translate Edwy's name, too, into Latin.

I paid the carter and thanked the villagers but stayed there with Nerian into the evening and watched the sun sink low until it went below the top of the sandstone cross, creating the effect of a halo above it and tinting the yellow-grey stone into ruddiness. I remembered Cuthbert's words about the beauty of God's Creation and made the sign of the cross in imitation of the shape we'd erected and meditated upon the blessing of true friendship.

EIGHT

THE NEW KING WAS INSTALLED WITH NO OPPOSITION, HIS accession greeted with favour by our northern neighbours who preferred him to a younger more warlike ruler. Different in this respect from his immediate predecessors, Aldfrith was welcomed also by the leading churchmen as a philosopher-king because of his renowned learning. Among the bishops to look favourably on his investiture was Cuthbert—some say he was a cousin to the king on his Irish side but I do not believe this. Whatever the truth behind the king's ancestry, nobody can doubt that his reign brought a period of prolonged prosperity and a revival of interest in literature and the arts.

If we had a philosopher-king, on a personal level, I was developing my philosophy of what I like to think of as *oneness*. To explain, I would attribute my notions to the profound influence on me of Bishop Cuthbert, my mentor, but also to the absence of liturgy in the village of Riding. My Church was the Outdoors and, when at work, my trade was conducted in silence and concentration. Most of my communication with others apart from seeking advice on leather-working from my father came when our customers passed by to collect their completed wares. Other than that, regular meetings with Nerian provided social contact. They gave me an opportunity to pass on what I had gleaned from Cuthbert. But with Nerian, I did not express my understanding of life, preferring not to deviate from what Cuthbert had taught me, for fear teaching him in error.

I believed there was nothing erroneous in my personal theories because they coincided well with Cuthbert's contemplative appreciation of Nature in all her glory. Like the good bishop, I had found a peaceful place to sit and reflect on my surroundings. In my case, it was the bole of an oak tree standing by the roadside twenty paces removed from Edwy's Cross, as I named it. The likelihood was that some fungal disease had afflicted the roots at the base of the trunk, causing swelling that with time blended perfectly with the bark of the tree to create a surprisingly comfortable seat for anyone disposed to rest his back against it. I had sat on this 'seat' since childhood whenever I passed by but in adulthood, I came every day before sunset to meditate on the world around me.

It was not long before the sighting of a black redstart with my admiration for that pert creature that I developed the idea that everything is composed of the same substance. Whether one thinks of it as spirit or consciousness is of no importance. What matters is the realisation that an apparent separation among individual creatures and plants is an illusion. In reality, everything is one. I should have liked to discuss my ideas with the bishop but, in truth, I was too contented with my life and dreaded moving to anywhere that might threaten its stability. As I gazed upon the busy meanderings of a bumblebee or flinched as a swallow swooped straight towards me on the lane before soaring at the last second, I knew most profoundly that the same basic essence permeates everything that exists—we are all part of the same whole.

I remember Cuthbert telling me that we should all look with wonder on the world as if through the eyes of a child, seeing things as if for the first time. I tried to live my life that way and found that it made me a calm, patient person, well-liked or even well-loved by family and friends. Only when I was much older—and I don't want to get too far ahead of myself—did I realise, without Cuthbert's help, that this was the state of grace he had spoken about.

—————

RIDING, SUMMER 687 AD

ANYWAY, two years went by with me in this regular untroubled existence, when, one evening, a familiar face appeared at the workshop.

"Aella, I find you well! And this must be your father. Greetings!"

It was the monk from Lindisfarena who had asked directions to my home more than two years before. I led him outside and offered a beaker of ale. Strangely, I didn't want to share his news, not even with my father.

"Brother, I am pleased to see that you too look hale and full of cheer. But what brings you to our humble dwelling? Do you have tidings of my friend, his Grace, the Bishop?"

He smiled in a way that puzzled me as much as his words. Did I detect sorrow in the smile?

"Well, yes and no. That is, Aella, he is rarely seen on Lindisfarena, for Bishop Cuthbert has resumed his austere life as a hermit on one of the inner isles. He lives in a cave and meditates, seldom receiving anyone. When he makes a rare appearance at the abbey, I note how he has aged. For a man of little more than fifty winters, he carries the years badly, I'll be frank with you, I fear that he will not see out many more Yuletides, such is the mortification of his poor body and the deprivation he endures."

I must have looked stricken because he seized my arm and smiled,

"Be not sorrowful, brother, for Cuthbert is deeply happy in the company of God alone and I am here today on his behalf and that of King Aldfrith."

That made me sit up. The last thing I wanted was to be called to arms. I was still wrestling with the meaning of his words...on *whose* behalf, Cuthbert's or God's? It wasn't clear, but the monk went on to explain why he had tramped here from Lindisfarena. He took a small piece of parchment, about three and a half by five inches from within his tunic. I could see at once that it was covered in beautiful handwriting in black ink. He handed it to me and I understood at a glance that it was in Latin. I had not learnt to read that language, struggling enough with my own tongue, as I am a craftsman not a scholar.

"Do you recognise it, Aella?"

I looked apologetic,

"I cannot understand Latin, brother."

"Ah, no, of course not. Well, this is the first page of the Gospel according to St John."

That meant something to me and forgetting I was not alone, said,

"*In the beginning was the Word, and the Word was with God, and the Word was God.*"

The monk threw his arm around my shoulder and pulled me closer.

"Exactly! Well done, Aella! I confess you surprise me."

I smiled into his beaming face.

"Bishop Cuthbert taught me. It's his favourite gospel. He told me that the Apostle produced a revelation straight from Heaven."

"And that is why I am here, Aella. King Aldfrith, knowing that it is Cuthbert's best-loved gospel, ordered the monks to write it out for him and in the last year we have done so. He reached down into his pack, which hitherto I had not noticed and pulled out a package bound with a leather thong.

"In this bundle are all the pages, they are the fruit of many long days scribing. The first page is also in there. This copy, he waved it disparagingly, contains an error and must be discarded. Those inside this parcel are all perfect but they require a home and that is your task, my friend."

I failed to grasp his meaning and he laughed at my bafflement.

"A home?"

"Ay, I mean you will bind the book and make it an exemplary cover in full respect of my brothers' labour of love."

I sighed with relief: this was no call to arms, but to work.

"I can do that, gladly."

"No commonplace piece mind, Aella, it must be worthy of a king's gift. That is why I have come to you."

"The king shall have my finest materials, wrought with all the skill I can muster, Brother."

"That is all I ask, my friend. With God's will, Cuthbert will have his gospel to read in his hermit's cell. Think how happy that will make him. Ah, before I forget..." he rummaged in his bag, "...the king sends you this."

The jewel flashed blood red in the evening sunlight from its clasp on a gold ring.

I gasped. When I had recovered, I turned it in my palm and then held it up to the setting sun.

"This is worth a fortune!"

"Ay, but the king knows you were his half-brother's godson. He said that Ecgfrith would have given you many gifts had he lived and this will cover the bequests of a lifetime. I'm sure you will repay him by producing a magnificent volume."

"Ay, that I will. Now, Brother, come indoors and savour my mother's food. I'll find you a bed for the night. You will not tramp the dark road after nightfall."

He protested out of good manners but was happy to accept our hospitality. Between mouthfuls of fresh bread and our home-produced cheese, he could not resist asking,

"When do you think it will be ready, Aella?"

I knew that to produce a perfect volume, my work would have to be meticulous and done only when I was rested and in the mood.

"I will not put a time on it, Brother. But I will make you a promise—it will take as long as is necessary to please, first myself, then, the king. When it is done, I'll bring it to you in Lindisfarena."

"A splendid answer, brother, but bear in mind, the bishop's health is precarious."

I reached inside my tunic and withdrew my clenched fist.

Looking around, I saw that my mother was pouring honey over a cake she'd baked especially for our guest.

"Mother, leave that be a moment and come here."

Curiosity on her face, because I never gave her orders, she drew near.

"Show me your fingers!"

She held out a hand flat and I knew it was perfect. Quickly, I slipped the ruby ring onto her middle finger. She had a working woman's solid hand and the ring was an exact fit. She gaped at it,

"What? Why, Aella?"

"Hush, mother! It is a gift from our king, Aldfrith. It is

yours, but do not show it outside the house, lest it might excite the unwanted attention of a scoundrel. It is beyond price."

Tears rolled down her cheeks and although she was speechless, I saw she was full of joy and gratitude.

"Aella, I know *why* you are Cuthbert's friend," the monk whispered, thereby giving to me a gift of equal value.

Before he left Riding the next morning, I took him to see Edwy's Cross. This was an excellent idea since he translated the Latin words for me. As he read the simple inscription, I memorised the translation. But what pleased me most was when he led me in prayer for the soul of my friend. I had prayed there for him many times, but it was comforting to have it done with the correct rite.

When we had finished, I promised again that I would start work on the book cover that day. What I meant was that I would think about it. My monk friend left the village with joy on his face. I returned to the workshop with sorrow on mine. I feared for Cuthbert's health and missed my old companion, Edwy, with a pang at the thought of him like the pain procured by a thorn pressed into the breast.

NINE

OFTEN MY BEST IDEAS COME TO ME AS I LIE HALF-AWAKE in my bed in the morning and so it happened on this occasion. After breakfast, I kissed my mother and hurried through the village to my favourite spot near Edwy's Cross. I sat on the tree bole and stared at the stonework. This was the idea that had come to me in bed. Right here in Riding, I had the template for my scrollwork. The interlacing around the panels was intricate. I gazed until my eyes were sore, understanding how it had been crafted. Only now did I begin to realise what a task the monk had set me to please the king. I knew that I was now as good if not better than father at tooling leather.

Where had I seen similar decorative work? Ah, ay, my mother's jewellery. Heaven knew, she possessed very little, but I recalled the shoulder clasp she used for her mantle. I would ask to study that when I returned for lunch. It was all very well having thought how to create the scrolled borders, but what would I put within the panels? I stared again at Edwy's Cross. Inside those two enclosed rectangles were the inscription and, in the other, the Nativity of Christ. Neither had any relevance to the cover I must produce.

I needed inspiration. What would the recipient of this book—Cuthbert—have done in my situation? He would have meditated. I stared at a honeybee busily flitting from floret to floret of borage, still in bloom in this late summer sunshine. My gaze went back to the stone cross. I had charged Master Almund with the task of portraying the Nativity, but the monk had given me no guidelines. All I knew was that the volume would be the Gospel of St John. What could I remember of those scriptures? Concentrating, I tried to recall Cuthbert's words on various occasions he had cited the work. One verse came to mind, where Christ compared himself to the vine. *I am the vine, ye are the branches.* I jumped up and hurried over to Edwy's Cross. Ay, there were the vine leaves, complete with grapes! What then if my central panel contained a vine? No, I dismissed that concept as not striking enough; nonetheless, I memorised the form of the leaves. Dejectedly, I went back to my seat and meditated. Sure enough, I began to formulate an idea. If you have a vineyard, you produce grapes, if you do that, you obtain wine. To drink it you need a beaker, but, nay, not a beaker—what did Cuthbert call it, the vessel he used in church? I could visualise it, ay, a chalice! So, if I designed one such as my central motif...it would represent Christ. But what of Saint John? He was an evangelist and The Church recognised three others, the bishop had told me that...but *ye are the branches...I cannot do that...but wait! What if I represent the evangelists as four grapes...the fruit of the vine!* Now I felt as if I was getting somewhere. All I needed was a scheme: the sequence of work I required to proceed.

I pondered; my poor brain striving as hard as the diligent honeybee still slaving around the blue five-petalled borage flowers. *Ah! The beauty of colour!* That inspired me to decide the start of my chain of tasks. First, I must choose the finest goatskin and cut it to size, it would be only slightly larger than the five and a half inches of the sample page; then I needed colour. My mother would know how to stain the leather. I had already decided it must be crimson and two small rectangles of goatskin would not require much dye. After that had been achieved, I would have to beg two needles from her because the pages in the bundle would have to be gathered and stitched together.

I stood and wended my way home to our workshop. My father was busy sewing the upper of a shoe to the sole. His needles were too big for the bookbinding I had in mind; nonetheless, it was time to confide in him.

"Father, that monk who came two days ago—"

"What about him?"

"Well, he came to give me a commission."

Oswin looked up and rubbed his eyes with the heel of his hand. He snorted, and said irritably,

"Are you going to talk to me in half-sentences, so that I must squeeze the information like water from a rag?"

"Sorry, father, you're right. I will explain. The monk was sent by King Aldfrith..." how he sat up! "...the king wants me to make a cover for a religious book—"

"Well, it would be, with him being a monk and all."

I laughed,

"You're right as ever; it's one of the most important Christian books and the king wishes it to be a gift for an eminent churchman."

"Then, you'll have to put all my teachings to good purpose, lad. If you need any advice..." He looked at me warily, not wishing to overstep the boundaries of our excellent relationship.

"Oh, I'm sure I'll be wittering at you endlessly, father. Let me begin at once: the book is small," I whipped out the page, "see, it won't require much leather, enough to cover pages like this. But I'll need to use our very best goatskin."

Father laid his needle on the bench and stood, crossed to the beam where the goatskins hung, ready for selection and cutting. His expert fingers tested the quality of the hide and after checking twice, lifted one and brought it over to me.

"This will be what you need, Aella." He deposited it on the bench and drew his finger across it. "Cut across here and you'll be at the softest, most workable piece. Make yourself a pair of boots from what's left. You could do with new ones for the winter. And we're not short of skins after your generous contribution."

"Glad to have helped, father. Ay, this is a fine skin, right enough. My thanks."

He watched with a critical eye as I took a fine-bladed knife and cut across the leather.

"There and there!" he pointed, unable to resist displaying his expertise.

I didn't comment and removed my two pieces, fingering the leather appreciatively. He had chosen well.

"Just taking these into the house, see you later."

Father looked puzzled but nodded and returned to his shoemaking. In the kitchen, my mother was peeling the apples she had picked the day before.

"Aella?"

She could see I was hesitating not wishing to interrupt her work.

"I need you to help me with these." I waved the two patches of leather.

"Why? What is it?"

Rapidly, I explained about the king's commission and how I needed to stain the goatskin leather red.

"I remember you dyeing linen red. I suppose you know how to do the same with these."

"Of course, but you'll have to help me collect the things I need."

I accepted eagerly.

"Go outside and unearth some madder root. You'll not need so much for that small amount of leather. Look for the new shoots, dig down there but go deep until you find the woody roots. Break them up. Here, fill this basket," she handed me a wicker trug, "the dye is just under the bark. You'll see that for yourself. When you've done that, go to the woods and find oak gall, I'll need enough to cover the bottom of this." She passed me a small round wicker basket. "When you've got everything, bring it back here and we'll prepare what you need.

"Where will I find madder?"

She looked at me and grinned,

"Typical! You're as bad as your father. Come with me!"

She led me to the back of the house and pointed. I planted it ten years ago. It's very invasive and I don't have the energy to deal with everything that needs doing around here." Her tone was truculent. "Go fetch a spade and dig here by this new shoot. I'll get back to my pie-making."

Grubbing out the roots wasn't difficult and I soon filled the basket. Luckily, I decided to show my mother before going to the woods.

"It's probably better to separate the red from the orange before they dry out, Aella. Fetch a knife and cut away the bark to remove this part of the root." She showed me. It meant wasting a significant amount of the root, but soon I had cut out many small cubes, which she considered sufficient.

"Pass me the pestle and mortar," she pointed to a high shelf. I reached it without a stool, she wouldn't have. "I'll need to grind it into a powder while you find the oak gall.

68

Finding oak gall was a simple matter, for if my neighbours were keen to collect acorns for their swine, they ignored and left the bitter gall that not even pigs deigned to eat.

My mother threw the gall and water in a pan to simmer them for half an hour; meanwhile, she made a paste with the madder root powder, mixed with chalk and water. When she was satisfied, she added water and boiled it all.

"How dark do you want the red, Aella?"

"The colour of dried blood."

I swear she shuddered,

"That dark? Then you'll need some wood ash. There's some in the hearth."

She bustled over and gathered some with a small shovel. This she sprinkled skilfully into the liquid and stirred it in. "Pass me that bottle, son."

When she opened it and splashed some liquid in, the pungent smell—vinegar—pricked my nose.

"That should do it! Now, find me a pan. Nay, bigger than that! Good, put your leather in it and set it on the table."

She took the oak gall liquor off the flame and carried it over to the leather, pouring it over the two patches and turning them over several times until she was satisfied.

"Why did you do that?" I had no idea.

"It's the gall, Aella, it soaks into the pores; without it, the dye will not bind but *with it* the colour will endure forever.

"How long must it steep?"

"It's ready."

She took the leather out of the liquor set the two small patches on the table and poured the bitter liquid on to the ground outside the door. Returning, she replaced the leather in the pan, brought the dye and slopped it carelessly over it.

"We'll leave them lie for half an hour. I hope the colour suits you."

I bent over to inspect her handiwork. The potion looked exactly like blood.

"Mother, you are a witch!"

She laughed and a wicked gleam came into her eye,

"You ought not to have said that, son, you have just forfeited your share of the apple pie."

"You know I didn't mean it! There's another thing you can do for me."

She muttered something I didn't catch, but I knew she had much to do.

"May I borrow your shoulder clasp? I won't need it till tomorrow."

"You'll have it when I've eaten *your* apple pie," she said with a twinkle in her eye.

When I came back to retrieve the leather, there was a delicious smell coming from the oven.

"I meant to say *sorceress*," I said with an exaggerated apologetic tone and a sorrowful expression.

"You'd say anything for apple pie!" She laughed gaily and I could scarce remember a day passed without hearing her laughter since I returned from the Pictish war.

The leather was a deep crimson colour and I thanked her fulsomely, deciding to wait a day or two before asking for yellow and blue dyes. I dared not risk my slice of the pie. In any case, I could not work the patches today: they needed to dry out completely.

"One last thing," I said, risking her wrath.

"What now!"

"I need two needles and a reel of stout thread."

And that had better be all for today, Aella, or I swear..."

Her words were lost as she disappeared behind the heavy drape. Taking the items from her, I kissed her cheek and didn't miss the fleeting flash of love before she repented and looked cross.

I returned to the workshop, where I threaded both the needles and opened the bundle the monk had left. I gathered a sheaf of pages, handling them with great care, using the needles to loop the stitches around each other in a figure of eight sewing pattern. I'd never done this before, rather performing by instinct, but the work was neat and strong. My ample experience of sewing shoes stood me in good stead. This sheaf finished, I set these pages aside and repeated the operation several times until I reached the end of the pile.

Oswin had feigned indifference, concentrating on his work, but I caught him glancing over more than once. When I knotted off the last of the stitching, he stepped over, picked up the sheaf from the top of the pile and bringing it close to his face, inspected my work. Replacing it, he said nothing but squeezed my shoulder. This was his way of giving high praise and knowing him, it pleased me well.

After a few minutes, I said,

"Father, I'll need two thin boards for the covers."

"Like these?" He grinned holding one up.

My mouth dropped open and I must have looked like the idiot, the fishmonger's boy at the Broomhaugh market.

"They're birch, I measured them from the hide you'd cut."

"Father, you're a sorcerer!" I cried, knowing there was no apple pie at stake.

He chortled and said,

"I expect you'll be asking for cord and glue next. The drill is over there!" He laughed again and once more I reflected on how good it was to be home. It hardly bore thinking about how close I had come to losing my life in Pictland, as Edwy had done.

I drilled a dozen holes in the birch front cover and four in the back one. Then I threaded cord into the holes, knotted it and cut it off. I glued the cord into position and decided that was all I could do for this one day. Anyway, Nerian would be along soon for his daily weapon practice. Just like his brother, he was better than me with the sword but could not match me at axe-wielding.

Today, after our exertions, I would tell him all I could remember about St John's Gospel. Nerian was showing great interest in Christianity. What appealed to him most was the thought of eternal life to spend with his brother, whom he missed more sorely than I. One thing I knew though was that if I had to fight again, there was no-one I'd prefer next to me in battle than Edwy's brother.

TEN

THE MOST DIFFICULT STAGE OF MAKING THE BOOK CAME when I had to apply the leather to the wooden board. The front cover was the delicate part because I knew the effect I wanted but to achieve it meant inventing a kind of plaster relief made of modelled clay packed with tiny scraps of leather. I spent days trying to get this right and abandoned four attempts before grudgingly admitting I would do no better than this last attempt. Pressing the clay down hard on the birch, I left it to harden and when it was ready, I stretched and pressed the dampened leather over it until it had taken the form of the chalice and leaves as I intended. Satisfied, I glued it down and with even weight over the whole surface, was pleased to see the details of the clearly defined entwined cord embossed in the leather. It was a matter now of tooling over the impressed shape.

Not that I was happy with my work; the craftsman's eye is very demanding and dwells on the slightest fault. Noticing one at this stage frayed my nerves as it was unthinkable to annul everything and start over simply for a minor defect. But my careless alignment of the holes for the cord meant that the lowest horizontal raised line wasn't straight, being higher on the left. I was angry with myself but when I pointed it out to my father, he laughed and said,

"Get away with you, Aella, when you've tooled the cover and used colour, it'll be so fine a work that nobody but you will notice it."

His words comforted me and made me determined not to rush the incision because haste is the craftsman's foe. I finished pressing and glueing and decided to do no more that day because I wanted to manipulate hardened covers that would not be compromised by movement.

When not working on the Gospel, I helped my father with his orders or by creating stock that later would be offered for sale at Broomhaugh market. Regarding stalls, I resolved to go to Hexham on my mother's advice. For days I had been steadily engraving the borderlines of the panels with a sharp pointed tool and, wishing to stain these lines bright yellow and blue, questioned her on how to produce the stains. Our conversation on the subject went like this:

"Bright yellow is difficult. I know how to make you a pale-yellow using weld."

"That might be acceptable for the back cover, but the front scrollwork must be bright yellow."

She frowned and I could almost hear her thoughts whirring,

"I'll need to go to Corbridge to obtain the woad for your blue and I can pick up the weld there, too. I recall that there are powders at Hexham market for dyeing. They bring them by ship from overseas. One of them has a strange name that I can't remember and it's made from ground crystals. They say it's deadly poisonous, so you won't want to be licking your fingers!" She giggled then looked apologetic, "You could accompany me to Corbridge and from there we can go the further league to Hexham. It'll make a change to have a nice day out," she tittered again.

I smiled at her fondly; my mother could be girlish sometimes although her hair was streaked with grey. Despite this, she had kept her figure and her impish humour that lit up her face, made her look younger than her fifty winters.

"The weather is set fair; we can go tomorrow, from here to Hexham is little more than five miles. If we leave early, even allowing for an hour in Corbridge, we can be there by midday."

"We'll pick our own woad—the leaves are like rabbit ears—there's a field full near Corbridge. That won't take long. As for the weld, it grows on chalky soil and at this time of year, we'll find it in rosettes and if we're lucky, some of it will have gone to seed. We can look for it by the old Roman stones. That might take us longer, Aella."

The drawstring bags we took with us were full within half an hour since collecting the weld was as easy as the woad. Both were available in abundance.

"We were lucky," my mother insisted, "it must be a good year for weld because it crops every two years."

I deferred to her knowledge but hoped that we would find the crystal with the name she could not recall, in Hexham, as obtaining the right shade of yellow was so important to me. I hadn't returned to the town since collecting Edwy's cross but its stench was as I remembered it. The market was bustling with folk and the cries of the traders and people jostling to get closer to the stalls annoyed me. Besides, I had no idea where to look for the powders my mother sought.

"It's like looking for a needle in a haystack here," I grumbled.

"Nay, be not grumpy, lad. Seek out a stall selling rolls of cloth."

"Like that one?" I was taller than she and pointed over the head of an old woman in front of me.

She could not see but I took her hand and we wove through the crowd until I brought her triumphantly to the stall with the many-coloured materials.

"Do you have any dye powders? I need yellow," she said.

The lank-haired fellow wore a black patch over his right eye and above and below it snaked a livid scar. Was he, like me, a former warrior?

"You'll be seeking weld, mistress," he flashed a broken-toothed smile.

"Nay, good man, I have a bag full of weld here. I'm after that powder that comes from ground crystal. The one with the odd name."

The one sound eye took on a shifty appearance and I caught it lingering on my money bag.

"Are you thinking of *orpiment*, mistress?"

"Ay, that's the name!" My mother cried out with her usual excitement.

"Or-pi-ment," he liked the sound of the name, dragging it out, "comes from a long way away, mistress. They say it's brought from a land of deserts far to the east. But look here, he reached for a roll of bright yellow cloth and began to unravel it. This here cloth was dyed with orpiment. You can't get this tint with weld, no, mistress, you cannot!"

Along with one or two other customers waiting impatiently, I started to lose patience.

"Do you have this powder or not?"

"Depends."

"On what?"

"On whether you're prepared to pay a fair price."

"Which would be what, exactly?"

The rascal made a show of scratching his head, "Depends."

"Now what!" I let him heed my annoyance by the way I spat out the words.

He looked uneasy. "On how much you want."

I looked helplessly at my mother.

"Just enough to fill my palm," she said brightly, sticking out her hand for him to judge the measure.

"That'd be three-sceattas-worth."

"Fair enough!" she chirruped looking at me for confirmation. I nodded and shook three of the small silver coins into my hand. The scoundrel reached out a paw eagerly.

"First, let me see the wares," I growled.

He glowered but bent down muttering and fumbled under the counter to produce a battered tin. Pulling off the lid, he stuck the container under my nose. The powder was bright yellow, right enough. Sufficiently brilliant to convince me.

I handed him the coins and he took a pair of shears to the yellow cloth, cutting a small square. Onto this he shook the agreed amount of powder and made the piece of material into a small sack, tied with a length of yellow ribbon.

"Bear in mind orpiment's a poison, friend."

"I will. Many thanks."

I led my mother away from the hectic market, behind the abbey to where the masons were working.

"Good day to you, Master Almund!"

We chatted for a while and I told him how he'd inspired my scrollwork on leather, which pleased him no end. He called for a flagon of ale and I was surprised when he convinced my mother to sup a beaker. Maybe it was that the long walk had given her a thirst.

On the road back home, it occurred to me that my next long march would be to Lindisfarena to deliver the completed gospel. However, I was in no hurry to undertake that particular journey for two reasons: first, I didn't want to spoil my masterpiece by rushing to beat the bad weather. The roads became difficult with the rain, hail and snow and winter, although not in the offing, would be by the time I finished my commission. Second, I wished to delay a possible encounter with King Aldfrith. In my experience, kings did not bode well for my future.

When the time came to stain my chain border, the orpiment produced the precise effect I sought. My mother's woad gave the pattern the blue interlacing I desired and the relief work of the cording and my central design made for the most effective cover anyone, including Aldfrith, might wish for.

My attention now turned to the back cover and, by now, as autumn turned into winter, I was working by candlelight. This was unpleasant because it strained my eyes since the flickering light cast deep shadows. Luckily, although no less precise, the incisions on the back were much simpler, with no raised elements as I'd decided on a geometric pattern of two stepped crosses made from small squares. With an outer border, similar to my mother's shoulder clasp scrollwork, stained blue, just like the grid, I made the vertical axis and the two horizontal axes pale yellow, using the weld dye.

By the time we entered the New Year, I was ready to complete my handiwork. It was time to insert the script. Having stitched the gatherings together, I used the same thread to attach the pages to the cover. This I did by sewing to the thicker cords that ran horizontally across the spine. Finally, I used glue to fix the parchment to the two boards of the cover. The threads holding the gatherings were knotted to them. The day I finished, it was rainy, gloomy January weather, so I had no sense of guilt at being unwilling to plod through the mud to the coast.

It troubled my conscience that my friend the monk must be on edge waiting for me to deliver the Gospel. I wondered how irritable King Aldfrith might be over the delay. Still, I was confident that all would be forgiven when he saw the beauty of my work. My father had pronounced it *a masterpiece* and something the like of which the world had never seen. But he was biased. I resolved that I would set off for Lindisfarena at the end of March. That would give me time to make my new boots.

This decision was unfortunate because when I reached the abbey of Lindisfarena the monk told me that I had just missed Cuthbert. The bishop had resigned his see the day before on the thirtieth day of the month and vanished as if from the face of the earth. He smirked, which told me that he suspected or, indeed, knew where the former prelate had gone. I was disappointed but determined not to impose myself on Cuthbert's solitude, so I didn't press the monk for the location.

When he saw the completed Gospel, he fell on his knees and praised God for guiding my hands; I hadn't thought of it like that, I admit, but could see merit in his attitude.

"You will come with me to deliver it to the king in person, Aella."

I protested vehemently, but he must have put it down to shyness because he would not hear my objections. The king was older than I'd imagined him and his red-golden hair had two grey wings at the temples. His beard was still its natural colour and his face, long and dignified, creased into a benign smile when the monk introduced me.

"Ah, Ecgfrith's godson. Do you love books, Master Aella?"

I felt my face burning,

"Sire, I admire them as objects, but I must confess—I know not how to read."

"Ah, that is remiss! I shall remedy that personally..."

Does he mean to be my teacher?

Of course, he did not. But first, he had to reprimand me.

"Why has it taken so long to bring the Gospel I commissioned? You see, Aella, the pity is, Bishop Cuthbert resigned from his see yesterday. Your arrival is welcome, but badly timed."

I reached into my bag and withdrew the Gospel extending it to him.

"Forgive me, Sire. I could not rush the work."

He was turning it in his hand, his expression inscrutable to my eye.

At last, he detached his gaze,

"So I see, Aella. It is a wonder! And I mean to repay you handsomely.

"Nay, Sire. You have already done so!"

"How is that?"

"The ring, Sire, that so enhances my mother's hand."

"Ah, the ruby ring! Your *mother's* hand! You are a remarkable man, Aella. I declare a great liking for you."

Breath rushed through my nostrils in relief.

"Heed me well," he said as if I had any choice, "yesterday, we had an important visitor—the learned Abbot Adomnan, the Abbot of Iona..."

How does this concern me?

He gave me a level stare, "I am minded to kill two birds with one stone. You were a warrior with Ecgfrith, I believe? You went to Ériu to fight beside Lord Berhtred, is that so?"

"It is, Sire."

His expression became thoughtful. Turning to my companion, he said,

"Brother, fetch a quill, ink and parchment."

The monk hurried away to do his bidding.

He gazed at me, his eyes more authoritative than friendly and without knowing why, my heart sank.

"Abbot Adomnan came expressly to plead for the return of

the captives brought here in slavery by Berhtred. I am minded to oblige the abbot, who is a saintly scholar. You, Aella, will escort them back to the island whence they came. I place you in command of twenty warriors. Go overland and sail from our western coast on the shortest crossing." He paused; I could tell he hadn't finished. Also, I remembered he had mentioned *two* birds. A discreet cough made him detach his gaze from my, no doubt troubled, face. The monk had returned with the requisite materials.

"Take this down, Brother, he began to dictate: "To my beloved cousin King Auisle, brother in God, King of Dublin..."

The monotonous scratch of the quill failed to lull me as I understood the nature of the missive—I was to be sent to this Irish king and thence to a monastery renowned for its learning to be instructed in reading and writing until such a time as I was proficient *according to their lights*, whatever that meant.

How long would I be away from home? My fear that kings bode ill was justified. But King Aldfrith smiled at me,

"Aella, this serves as recompense for the masterpiece you have brought here today, but my liking for you is extraordinary, here..." he wriggled a ring with a blue gem from his finger, "You, as well as your mother, must have a token of my love."

The king ordered me to return the next day to take charge of the captives and to begin my escort duties. The monk handed me the portentous letter and we bowed our way out.

"Look on the bright side, Aella, you will become a learned man and be able to read the Bible," said the monk.

I humoured him, but to be honest, I'd had enough of Gospels and the like. All I wanted was the opportunity to watch my parents grow old.

ELEVEN

KINGDOM OF BREGA, ÉRIU, SPRING 686 AD

WE MARCHED INTO THE FORMER TERRITORY OF RHEGED
with sixty hostages for most of whom this was their land of
origin. From the coast of this erstwhile kingdom, we boarded
our ships and sailed to the Isle of Man, which was also part of
Northumbria. The spring weather, as usual, was uncertain and
it changed so that we could not sail for three days since the
Irish Sea, waves enraged by the gales that swept from the
south-west, would have swamped our two vessels. Prudence
caused us to relinquish the first day of calm water, but we
embarked for Brega the following day.

As we entered the harbour, we saw armed men staring and
pointing at our ships. Our mission was peaceful but they were
not to know that. Slowly, we manoeuvred the vessels to the
quay and disembarked the hostages. The Irish warriors drew
near to understand what we were about. That was when
disaster struck me.

One of the older women captives began to shout, pointing
at me,

"Seize him! I know his face! This is one of the bastards who burnt our church and slew our menfolk. Not the others—only that one!"

I saw the angry expressions on the savage faces and in a trice, my axe was seized and my arms pinned behind my back as I was shoved forward to face what doom?

"String him up!" yelled the woman, her heart set on vengeance. Other voices among the hostages backed her up. Hope died in my breast as I watched the men of my escort shrug and return to the ships. I didn't blame them. Who was I to them? Nothing but a temporary commander, also, they were heavily outnumbered.

The local warriors pushed and shoved me into the town. I recognised it as one of the places we had ravaged two years before. They had rebuilt the houses and now directed me towards a larger building. I guessed it was the chieftain's hall and this intuition proved correct. Maybe, the headman of the village would decide my fate. I would try and plead my innocence, but the woman would surely denounce my presence on that punitive raid. Therefore, I could expect no mercy from a populace so badly wronged by Ealdorman Berhtred and our men.

The chieftain, as with many of his warriors, was a savage-looking red-haired individual. His expression became enraged when the woman, who claimed her husband's throat had been slit by the raiders, pointed her finger at me.

"Do you deny you took part in the attack on my people?"

"I do not, Lord. But I did not slay anyone."

"He's a liar! He's trying to save his filthy skin!" she shrieked and a chorus of "Ay-s" greeted her from the assembled hostages.

"It's enough that you took part, Saxon," said the headman, "you condemn yourself out of your own mouth. It is true that you have brought my people back unscathed, but back to what?

To tend to the graves of their husbands and fathers? Shall I be the one to refuse them justice? I insist you will pay for your crimes."

"Ay! Make him pay!"

The woman screamed these words then came to look me in the face, hers a mask of hatred. She stared hard and then spat straight at my eyes. Since my arms were pinned behind me, I could not wipe away the spittle.

"Take him and hang him from a bough until he's dead!"

"Wait!"

It was a male voice this time. I'd never heard it before but what he said amazed me.

"I know this man. I recognised him at once. It was he who saved my life on the day of the raid. He could easily have slain me; instead, he pushed me into the bell-tower and hid me from his blood-thirsty comrades. It is to him that I owe my life."

"Father, look closely, are you sure it is the *same* man?" said the headman.

The priest drew near and wiped the spittle away gently with a cloth.

"I swear before God that this is the man. Look at his face brothers and sisters: there is no wickedness there, nothing that a good wash wouldn't cure."

Relief flooded through me, but I was not safe yet. Would they heed their priest? Or would the desire for vengeance blind them? I knew not what expression to put on my face. I suppose instinct prevailed, for I smiled at the clergyman.

"Are you a Christian, brother?" he asked.

Unable to move my arms, I invited him, "Look inside my tunic, Father."

He understood and his fingers felt for the chain around my neck. Gently, he hauled out the cross that Ecgfrith had gifted me. Holding it between finger and thumb, he raised it for everyone to see.

"Look! This is our brother in Christ! You must not harm him and remember he saved the life of your priest." He turned to the scowling woman, "Daughter, can you not find forgiveness in your heart? This man is not your enemy, for he acted like a true Christian. Can you not do likewise and be blessed by the Lord?"

Tears rolled down her cheeks and she hung her head but raised it to nod her assent. My heart went out to her for her loss and I said,

"Mistress, I share your sorrow, but we have a new king and he is a good man: you need fear no more."

"Well spoken stranger," said the chieftain. "Unhand him! You spared Father Ciaran and that is more than enough to make you my honoured guest." His previously ferocious countenance broke into a toothy smile. The painful grip on my arm relaxed and became a clap on my back. Mixed with my relief was a new insight into the workings of the Holy Spirit. Not only had He inspired me to save the priest but He had moved the man to speak up for me—mysterious workings, but not so different from the wyrd my father so believed in.

How strange and volatile people can be! One moment they wished to execute, the next to befriend me. The cleric took me to his home, promising to return with me to dine with the chieftain and his closest men.

Wishing to find out about his guest from Northumbria, I was obliged to recount my life story and he was especially interested in the last two years after my re-entry from Pictland.

"So, you are a craftsman and from your account of King Aldfrith's appreciation, a highly skilled one," he mused

"I do my best, not that it's done me much good."

"How so, Aella?"

"In my experience, kings are to be avoided. Had King Ecgfrith not wreaked woe upon your people, my life would not have been endangered this day. Equally, Aldfrith sent me here and it is he who will keep me from my family."

"Why, will you not return to them on the morrow?"

"I would that it were so, Father, but my king has commanded me to take a letter, which I bear on my person, to the King of Dublin. Is his court far from here?"

Father Ciaran chortled but still looked intrigued by my tale.

"Nay, it is fewer than fifteen leagues from here. If you have coin for a boatman, you can be there in a matter of hours, for it is near the coast."

"Then that is what I'll do. I am commanded to remain in Ériu until I can read and write. King Auisle will send me to a centre of learning."

"I'll wager he'll dispatch you to Clonmacnoise, where the best scholars in Christendom congregate. It is a wonderful place, Aella, close to the great River Shannon. I would envy you if it were not a mortal sin!"

"How long will it take me to learn to read and write?"

He laughed so hard I almost felt offended, but he wiped a tear from his eye and said,

"You set a fine riddle, my friend. Most of all, it depends on your thirst for learning; then, upon what your teachers decide. They may choose to teach you only Latin, but if they wish you also to learn Greek, it will make the task harder and longer. On the other hand, writing should not be a problem for your craftsman's hand and eye."

By now, my face was glum as I imagined a lifetime of study stretching ahead. One consolation was his account of Clonmacnoise, which seemed from his description a veritable paradise on earth.

"Of course, Clonmacnoise is not the only centre of monastic learning in Ériu, Aella, we are blessed with many learned scholars. The sons of kings and chieftains come from afar to study in this land."

There was no point in setting my heart on a place I'd never seen. That was foolish; so, I decided to leave my destination to divine providence. An appreciation of that concept was formulating in my head and I confessed it to my new friend.

"I told you about Bishop Cuthbert and how I had learnt of Christianity and was baptised by him, well, I believe I have been brought to Ériu for a purpose. It's not just to learn to read and write, I think it is much deeper, but I know not why."

The priest gave me a joyful grin,

"Oh, but you will know in God's good time, Aella. I too suppose He has a plan for you. From everything you have told me—your circumstances are too extraordinary for it to be otherwise."

We chatted for hours and I became increasingly aware of how true Christians lead their lives surrendering themselves with faith to God's will. I vowed to myself that henceforth I would do the same and trust that He would lead me home to my loving parents in His good time.

By the time the sun set and the hour came to stroll to the hall, we were firm friends and the idea of living in this land didn't oppress me as before. To seal this, I enjoyed a delicious meal the sea provided. Father Ciaran started proceedings by saying grace before we tucked into platters laden with oysters. When I had a dozen empty shells on the table in front of me, a steaming large sea bass was placed before me. I enjoyed it so much that I hoped fervently to eat this type of fish on further occasions. The priest shared some of my story with the chieftain, who on learning that I had to visit his overlord in Dublin, immediately arranged for a boatman to take me on the morrow. We finished the meal cracking walnuts and I found them a better accompaniment for the strong ale, which I'd drunk sparingly with the delicate fish.

My beaker now went to war! The amber liquid made my head spin after a while, so I needed to be skilful to make it appear I was still keeping pace with the red-haired giant opposite me. The conclusion that these people were more hospitable, and even harder drinkers, than the Northumbrians was inescapable. My day had gone from stark horror to mellow delight and my apprehension about the future to healthy curiosity.

Father Ciaran came down to the quay to bid me farewell.

"Now, Aella, promise you will not leave these shores without passing by to greet me. Promise in the name of friendship!"

I was pleased to do so and departed light-hearted as if on an adventure. As the sail filled and we bore away out of the harbour, I looked back and he waved and I blessed him for having saved my life. I scrambled to the rear of the boat near the steersman and asked what fare he would require.

"Nay, man, Lord Dunan has seen me right. It's taken care of. A couple of hours with this steady breeze," he looked at the sail and smiled, "and you'll be in Dublin: or *Duiblinn* as they call it in the town. The name means *Black Pool*, you know, there's a dark tidal pool where the river meets the harbour. Anyhow, you'll see it for yourself soon enough. It's only five minutes on foot from there to King Auisle's palace that overlooks it."

Like the other men of his community, he was voluble and good company. The time passed pleasantly and, after nosing the boat into the dark pool, he moored and insisted on accompanying me to the hall. Outside, once more I tried to offer him coin for an ale in a Dublin inn, but again, he refused, this time with a broad grin.

The document I was carrying was enough to gain me admittance to the hall; of course, I was forced to leave my axe and seax at the door in the guard's custody. I smiled to myself because he had let my most lethal weapon pass—the throwing knife I had claimed from the old grinder's chest. Still, I had no intention to use it. At the thought, I smiled again.

Inside the hall, there were many people assembled and I had no idea who was King Auisle since there was no throne and nobody seemed more the centre of attention than any other. I wandered around the sides of the great hall, admiring the drapes, all the while looking uncertain. I assume my air of aimlessness attracted the curiosity of a woman dressed in finery.

"Hail, stranger," she smiled and wrinkled her nose charmingly as if perplexed, "you are not of these parts, what brings you to Duiblinn?"

"I seek audience of King Auisle."

"Ah, my cousin!"

My wits were sharp, not befuddled by ale as the evening before, so, smartly I said,

"Perhaps then, you are a cousin to my king."

"Who may that be?"

"Aldfrith of Northumbria."

She laughed gaily and I could not help admiring her prettiness,

"Aldi!" her laugh tinkled cheerily and brought a smile to my lips, "How shrewd of you, stranger, do you have a name? Aldi and I were playmates and, truly, we *are* cousins."

"My name is Aella and I have a document for the king from your cousin."

Then, Aella, I will take you to him. You'll never find him in this throng as you know him not."

She glided through the assembly, people deferentially moving to ease her swan-like passage until we arrived at a group of four men.

"A moment of your time, Sire. Nay, not for me, but the charming Aella, here."

I nodded in gratitude and began a stumbling thanks, but she steered me towards the king. He was a head taller than his companions and possessed astute, penetrating blue eyes. Differently from the other men in the hall, his beard was close-clipped and his lips fully visible. This orderliness extended to his well-manicured nails, which I noticed when I handed over the document. The speed of his reading confirmed my impression that he was notably intelligent.

"Welcome, Aella, godson of Ecgfrith of blessed memory, and it seems, beloved of Aldfrith. You must dine with me this evening, for I will present you to a scholar I greatly esteem."

I plucked up courage, after all, he had spoken well of me, and asked,

"Is he from Clonmacnoise, Sire?"

He beamed at me and around his companions as if sharing a joke, I hoped not at *my* expense,

"You see, my friends, the fame of our monastic centres has reached foreign shores." He turned back to me, "No, not from Clonmacnoise, but a place of equal renown. You shall learn about it at dinner. I expect you will need to find an inn, Master Aella. Return at sunset, I await you."

I thanked him, bowed, and left the hall, regaining my weapons at the entrance. Turning to the guard, I said, "Your king has invited me to his table this evening. How shall I enter, for I have no document?"

He studied my face and said,

"I'll not be here at that hour, but I'll tell my comrade. What name do you go by?"

"Aella."

He was as good as his word. A glance at me from the relief guard, my name given, and I strode unimpeded into the hall. The scene that greeted me was completely different from the afternoon's crowded hall. Where the throng gathered before, now tables were laid and crowded with people. At the end of the hall, raised on a dais, was the king's table and my eye detected one empty seat opposite the monarch. I strode along an aisle separating the tables, never once removing my gaze from the king. He looked up, saw my approach and gestured me to the vacant place...and to what unimaginable fate?

TWELVE

DID I SAY UNIMAGINABLE FATE? THAT EVENING WAS TOO close to surreal for my poor brain to cope with and it caused me to anguish about what destiny awaited me in Ériu. Yet, it began well enough with King Auisle providing a warm welcome.

"This is our friend Master Aella, the finest leather-craftsmen in Northumbria. He has come to us to seek illumination in our monasteries." As he said this, I noticed he looked hard at the man sitting to my right, and he proceeded with an introduction, "Master Aella, by your side sits one of the most learned men in Christendom, Mo-Chuaróc moccu Neth Semon, Abbot of Les Mór Mo Chutu—or what we call Lismore!" With that, he howled with laughter and added, "You may find our native tongue a little difficult to master, my friend," and roared with mirth again, most at the table joining in, to be weirdly echoed by the people at the tables below and at my back, which could have heard nothing but the guffaws. So, my strange experience commenced.

"Let the food be brought, the feasting begins!" the king bellowed.

"You are fortunate, Sire," said the abbot, "for this is the Lenten period of abstinence, but as today is *Thursday*, whereas were it yesterday or tomorrow I could not have partaken."

This was my first inkling of the intricacies of Christian dogma, with its unchallengeable convictions. Now the master of orthodoxy to my right turned his attention to me. His beard was long and white, so I gathered he was advanced in years. It fascinated me how it bobbed up and down as he spoke, but I could not allow any distraction, as I knew I would need to maintain my concentration.

"You are a practising Christian, are you not, Master Aella?"

I pondered for a moment how best to answer, feeling all eyes on me.

"Well, Father Abbot," I hoped this was the correct form of address, anyway, it didn't seem to offend him, "I am a Christian, but our village has neither church nor priest, but at my expense, I arranged for the crafting and erection of a stone cross, with a carving of Our Lord's Nativity, where the entry roads to our settlement meet."

"It was a fine thing you did, my son. But surely you can walk to the nearest church?"

"There is the Abbey at Hexham, but as my mentor, Bishop Cuthbert explained to me—"

"Cuthbert! I knew him as a youth in Dùn Barra! So, you know Cuthbert, and what did he say?"

I smiled with fond memory,

"He taught me that the world around us can be our Church and that our hands can serve the Lord as well as, if not better than, our tongues."

The abbot gazed at the king,

"Hark at these wise words, Sire but everyone beware heresy! The Church is the only depository of the Truth! I am sure Master Aella realises that men cannot worship trees or false idols..."

I snapped out of my reverie; the abbot was waiting for a reply.

"Of course not, Father Abbot, but I believe a man may gaze on a majestic oak tree and see therein the magnificence of the Creator's work."

"In this, you are not mistaken, my son, but our king says you have come here *to seek illumination in our monasteries.* Not just illumination, I hope, because you should also search for truth. Much as I admire Bishop Cuthbert," with his knife, he toyed with the fish on his platter, "he, like others who give overly credence to the Church of Rome, has strayed into error." He impaled a piece of fish and carried it to his mouth, where with a fascinating flash of white whiskers, it disappeared. He gulped it down to continue his disquisition, which became increasingly odd. "Aella, there are but ten days to Easter Sunday and as you know, the significance of that holy day is the *cardinal prop* of our faith." His bright green eyes latched on to mine, with an expression of exaltation, "The *exact* date of Our Lord's resurrection is of fundamental importance and it is here that we must take a stand against Rome!" He went on to talk about embolistic months and intercalary ones and blue moons. He seemed like a man possessed and quite lost me with the strange terms he used. He had caused the king to lose interest, too, who was now talking about other matters with a flame-haired man next to him.

I strove to pay attention to the abbot's discourse, not wishing to incur the disapproval of the man whose abbey was surely writ large in my future. He was saying,

"...So, you see, Aella, the *only* Paschal cycle we ought to give credit to is the Cyrillian. Do you know how it came about?

Of course, I bloody don't. Curse Aldfrith for sending me here!

I admitted I did not, which pleased the old monk no end. How he liked the sound of his own voice!

"Well, there lived an abbot in Egypt. He founded the Monastery of Baum in the period soon after the time of the Apostles' sufferings. His name was Pachomius and he is considered a saint by the Church. Not wishing to fall into error about the calculation of Easter, he and his monks prayed to the Lord for enlightenment. The Lord sent an angel to the saint and ordered him to write down according to his dictation so that he would thenceforth encounter no error in the solemnity of Easter and would know the moon of the first month in each common and embolismic year. What do you think of that, my son?"

What do I think? What am I supposed to think of such matters? I don't even know what some of the words mean. But I'll have to keep him happy.

"Surely, Father, nobody may dispute the word of the Lord sent by an angel?"

"Exactly!" he stamped the handle of his knife on the table, causing all conversation around us to cease. He had the grace to look apologetic and astonished me by saying, "Sire, you are consigning me a simpleton, whose simplicity makes him the wisest of men!"

Damn it! He's calling me a simpleton.

The king roared with laughter,

"Look at his face! By all the saints, Abbot Mo- Chuaróc only you could make a man disconsolate with a compliment!" The king grinned at me, his face reddened by the quantity of ale he'd supped, "Do not be dismayed, Aella, you will accustom yourself to monastic ways. The abbot meant no offence."

"Good Heavens, no!" said the abbot as if the idea had never

occurred to him, "Our Lord says that we all, every one of us," he looked around belligerently, "must be as pure as little children. Master Aella has a wondrous simplicity—we...I... must be careful never to deprive him of it."

The others at the table were rapidly losing interest in the old man's burbling, but I did not have that luxury. The abbot was like a ratter dog with its prey between its teeth, and Easter was a subject dear to his heart.

"What was I saying? Ah, the Cyrillian calendar! Now thanks to a misguided Pope by the name of Leo, we have a dispute. He ordered a calculation by Victorius of Aquitaine, a mathematician, who arbitrarily inserted embolismic months and intercalated days—"*and*," his voice became indignant, "they have the audacity to profess that they follow the decrees of the Council of Nicea..."

It was at this point that he lost me and I began drinking heavily. The abbot might just as well have been talking in Greek for all I understood him. He was still chuntering as I refilled my beaker, "... but where is that written down? I'd like to read it! There is no transcript of the Council referring to Easter. You see Aella..." the use of my name refocused my attention, "there can be a difference of *thirty-five* days between the two calendars."

"B-but that's five weeks!" I said, genuinely shocked.

"Exactly!" Thank goodness he had laid down his knife, no table thumping this time, "I think that you, Aella, have been sent to us to achieve great things!" And that was the first clear-cut remark I'd heard from him in a while and made up for all the gibberish I'd hitherto endured. I hoped that my stay at Lismore Abbey, not officially confirmed yet, would not involve me having to learn the intricacies of the lunar calendar. I was happy to take his word that Easter Sunday would be April 15 this year.

Now the confirmation of my acceptance into the monastery came. The abbot caught the king's attention.

"Sire, is it your intention to place Master Aella under my tutelage?"

The king scrutinised both our faces before pronouncing,

"Ay, that is what I wished to request of you, Abbot Mo-Chuaróc? How does it suit you?"

"Oh, very well, Sire, I believe Aella has been sent to us for a purpose, and we must obey God's will in all things."

"That's settled then," the king belched, his face was now grown quite ruddy. He didn't seem to want to extend the conversation, simply grinning and nodding before filling both our vessels, raising his horn to knock it against my beaker, sloshing decent ale from mine onto the table.

I had no idea where Lismore was and only later realised that it was south-central Ériu and not so far from the sea. Thank goodness the abbot didn't wish to honour Easter by travelling the length of the country on a donkey. Since Lismore was near the coast, we sailed to a port called Youghal where we transferred to a peculiar round wicker-framed boat covered in hides, called a *curragh*, whose boatman paddled us from the estuary up the wide River Avonmore, its name meaning *the great river*, which was deep enough to bring us close to Lismore. We walked the last half mile and the abbot, who I must say had been a better company on the voyage than in the king's hall, probably because he left matters of doctrine there and preferred to share the wonders of nature with me. Thanks to Cuthbert, for him I was able to distinguish kittiwakes, fulmars, petrels and shearwaters and together we admired the colourful puffins, and the drab grey seals bobbing in the sea or basking on the rocks.

When we disembarked, at the sight of the abbey, he returned to the clerical mode and pointed out a building, on a hill overlooking the town and the river valley, steeply rising from the south bank of the Avonmore.

"There stands the abbey that my mentor founded, the late lamented Mo-Chutu macFinaill, Aella, about the time I was born. Some churchmen retain he lived as a saint and I am sure he will be canonised as Saint Mochuda, just you see.

What I saw was that they all had very difficult names. How would I ever remember them? Also, I wondered what monastic life would mean for me. I could deal with monotonous routine but nothing as complicated as—what had the abbot called them? —*intercalated* days. Did it matter to me that Easter fell on a precise Sunday? Honestly not, the dabchick bobbing about on the surface of the Avonmore spoke more to me about the presence of God, making me wonder whether I was an incorrigible pagan! On the other hand, the abbot was the latest in a series of churchmen to see something of a calling for me— could they *all* be wrong? I supposed not, but if only I had a glimpse of what that calling might be.

THIRTEEN

WHATEVER MISGIVINGS I HAD ABOUT BEING FORCED TO
become a monk were swiftly allayed as I encountered the
reality of Lismore Abbey. Before setting foot in the place I had
no idea of how many laymen frequented its corridors. One of
the first things Abbot Mo-Chuaróc told me as he organised
sleeping for me was that my residence in the monastery would
be conducted in respect of the regulations for lay visitors. This
was a relief because it meant my days would not be governed
by bells and services. Of the nine divine offices, laymen were
expected to attend Prime and Vespers, which effectively
corresponded to dawn and dusk and this suited me very well,
as I was ever an early riser. It would also be an opportunity to
learn more about the faith. After consenting to baptism, apart
from my conversations with Bishop Cuthbert, I had not
attended services, both for lack of a church and the absence of
desire on my part.

Intrigued to find out about the other laymen within the
monastic walls, I soon discovered that they were mostly the
sons of chieftains and kings. To the fore among my

99

misapprehensions had been the notion that I was in some way specially selected for individual tutelage, perhaps with Abbot Mo-Chuaróc himself. To disabuse this idea, a monk charged with taking me to my first class led me to a group of young men assembled and seated in a stone-walled chamber with benches and tables.

"Attention everyone! This is Aella Oswinsson who joins us today from Northumbria."

I smiled shyly at the expressionless faces and sat obediently next to a muscular fellow with hair the colour of chestnuts. He grinned and nodded a greeting, which was the first sign of amiability in that cold room.

Our teacher was a tall, thin sallow-faced monk, whose tongue, I soon learnt was sharp and witty and this together with his profound learning, was enough to maintain a rigid discipline born out of respect. We were to learn Latin from him and so began my introduction to declension: the nominative, vocative, accusative and so forth. It was alien and I feared I would not grasp it, but the monk, Brother Senach, cared for each student and had the patience and the insight not to lose a single one. Thus, thanks to his clear teachings, I caught up and surpassed many of my classmates.

First impressions are not always reliable, but my chestnut-haired companion confirmed my early perception of him. He declared that his name was Lugaid Uá Broíthe, along with an explanation that Uá referred to the *tuath* or tribe that he belonged to. The Kingdom of Munster possessed Lismore and Lugaid proudly stated that his family was one of the oldest in the historic Kingdom of Osraige, which only recently had reasserted its independence from the much greater Munster. He was the son of a chieftain, who had played an important part in this political outcome.

We spent much of our free time together and I believe it

pleased him to have a Saxon friend who was also older than himself. Our conversations were wide-ranging and many of them conducted in attempts at Latin, to improve our proficiency in that language.

After a year had passed in the silence of Lismore Abbey, so conducive to learning, we were issued with pens and ink and taught to form the letters. I developed an aptitude for calligraphy that should not have surprised anyone, my hand and eye being trained to coordinate for precise incision. I can vaunt being the best in the class at writing if not at Latin. I also found reading singularly easy, rarely stumbling, like others, over the words. A report on our progress was written down by Brother Senach and consigned to the abbot.

———

LISMORE ABBEY, KINGDOM OF MUNSTER, APRIL 687 AD

AS USUAL, at the end of the first year, Abbot Mo-Chuaróc summoned students individually to discuss their progress. Lugaid came out of what we thought of as the mysterious *sanctum sanctorum* with a reassuring wide grin—but then, I knew he was a clever student. My turn came and I pushed back the heavy oak door and entered an austere chamber that did honour to the abbot's vows of poverty and abstinence. The only trappings of luxury in the bare room was a painting that immediately caught the eye. When I saw the gold leaf-painted image of Christ in Majesty, a Gospel in his hand, I instinctively made the sign of the cross. This met with the instant approbation of the abbot.

"Do you like it, Aella? It came from Constantinople and let's say – er – it is an indulgence of mine."

I muttered incoherently that I did, being rather more

concerned that my progress as a student might not please him. I need not have worried because his interest in his students went well beyond their performance in the classroom.

"Aella, I have been particularly pleased by your attentiveness at our services and I noted with approval your instinctive reaction to my icon." He nodded towards the painting—I had no idea they were called *icons*. "Now, regarding your progress with your studies, Brother Senach writes that your Latin is coming along well but that you must pay more attention to the regular verbs. He is satisfied with your competent reading and your writing apparently is outstanding. As with other students who have done well, I am going to quote you an important dictum: *Mens sana in corpore sano*.

"A healthy mind in a healthy body" I translated, eager to impress.

"Quite so! It was a great Roman poet, who lived six hundred years ago, Decimus Iunius Iuvenalis, and he formulated that concept. It is a fundamental truth, Aella, and that is why you and your fellow students with optimum results are granted a three-week break from study. Well done, my son, you may go! Please send me..." he consulted a list, "...Colum MacBroian."

Colum and I did not get on. I suspected he was jealous of my friendship with Lugaid as I could think of no other reason. I stood outside in the corridor but my hesitation was not on account of any antipathy for Colum, but rather perplexity regarding the three-week break. I began to amble towards the others lost in thought sufficient to alert Lugaid, who called,

"Why the long face Aella? Have you been reprimanded for your poor efforts?" Everyone laughed since they knew I was a good student.

I made no reply but grinned and said,

"Your turn, Colum."

He nodded, grunted something unintelligible and slouched towards the abbot's quarters.

Lugaid linked arms and we moved away from the others, "So, what's the matter?"

As usual, his tone was kind and I looked into his concerned grey eyes.

"Ach! It's this blessed three-week break."

"Why, aren't you pleased to have some time off studying?"

"It's not that Lu-i; it's that it's too short a time to travel to Northumbria to see my folks. By the time I get there, it'll be time to come back."

"Mmm, you're right. I know! Why don't you come home with me? You can meet my family and stay with us. It'll be great!"

I looked into his eager face and smiled, but I had to refuse.

"I can't impose on their hospitality, Lu-i, besides, you'll have missed them and want to be with them, not with a gloomy old Saxon leather-worker."

"Idiot! You are neither gloomy nor old, and my family is used to entertaining guests. They do it all the time, you'll be lost in the crowd!"

Relief washed over me, I wanted to go with Lugaid, but only if I'd be truly welcome.

Thankful for the stout boots I'd made myself, we arrived in his home village of Ardfinnan after tramping for six hours. With just one of the six leagues still to be walked, I pointed in the distance to a building on a hill.

"Is that your father's hall?"

Lugaid chortled and clapped me on the back, "You can go there if you want, but I wouldn't advise it."

"Why not?"

"Because, my dear friend, it's a monastery founded by

Finian Lobhar. Do you know what *lobhar* means in our language?"

I confessed I did not.

"Well, it means leper. Yon monastery has a leper colony—it was founded by Finian the Leper."

I shuddered, "Poor devils!"

The village lay by a river my friend called the Suir. "Good for eels," he said. That pleased me, as I hoped for a good eel stew, a favourite dish of mine.

At the centre of the settlement, of seven farmsteads, stood the chieftain's hall, hard by the church. Both were wooden structures and as we approached them, children ran squealing and pointing at us, in truth more at Lugaid, who grinned and ruffled the hair of a boy who came too close. Some of the children ran to announce his arrival, bringing their mothers to greet the chieftain's son. I could see from their deference how esteemed his father must be.

We strode into the hall and before we had gone three paces, a woman's voice cried with delight,

"Lu-i! My son! You are home, at last! Ser-la! Come, your brother is home!"

Sherlaith was a beauty; she stood as tall as her sibling although I judged her some years younger. She rushed into his arms and covered his cheeks with kisses. Then she stopped, remembering that her brother was not alone and, wriggling in his embrace, turned to smile and greet me.

Breaking free of his grasp, she fixed me with the same grey, but larger, eyes than her brother's,

"Will you not present your companion, Lu-i?" she said tossing back a mane of the same chestnut hair but more lustrous than his. I supposed she brushed it every day, whilst I couldn't recall Lugaid ever brushing his.

"Mother, Ser-la, this is Aella, my best friend and he's the

greatest Saxon leather-worker ever and the finest writer in our class!"

"Lady, your son is given to exaggeration," I said blushing.

"Not overmuch!" Sherlaith said, making the flush deepen. "But tell us, Master Aella, where do you call home?"

I liked her at once, as I find people who are interested in others, agreeable, especially if they are polite females with well-formed cheekbones, an oval face and full lips. I realised I was staring at her, struck by her beauty and flushed at her quizzical smile.

"*Er,* it's only a small village on a river in Northumbria," I said, not meaning to, but sounding apologetic.

"Do not apologise, young man, their mother said, "for ours is *only* a small village on a river!"

They all laughed and I felt foolish, reddening once more.

"My word!" Sherlaith teased, "but you *do* blush easily, Master Aella. "I fear you are too modest for your own good."

I felt my cheek and found it hot to the touch.

"I'm always like this when I meet new people, especially —" I bit my tongue to save making an even greater fool of myself.

But the vixen would not let it pass, "Especially..." she tilted her head coyly, "...do finish what you were saying."

My thoughts raced, but my wits are sharp, "Particularly when they are the family of a dear friend."

"I think we shall become *dear friends*, too, Aella!" she said archly.

Damnation my face is burning again!

Lugaid cleared his throat, smiled at his mother and said, "Where is my father?"

I felt sure he was saving me from the talons of his sister and I was grateful.

"Gone to market at Clogheen. He should be back before

long," his mother said.

"Well, mother, sure you'll not make us wait till his return for an ale. It's been a long march!"

Now it was her turn to have a flaming face. She looked downcast, but clapping her hands summoned a young woman, who bobbed first to Lugaid then to me, before dashing off to do her mistress's bidding.

"Come!" said the lady of the village, "sit and recount your tales. The days can be so dreary without company, can they not Ser-la?"

Frankly, I could not imagine any day being dull in the presence of the two lovely women and gallantly said as much, earning instant acceptance into the family.

I was pleased that my friend's mother wanted to know everything she could extract from us about our life at Lismore Abbey as this removed attention from me for a while. The ale was good and strong; I decided it was twice-brewed.

I noticed with pleasure, and not a little vanity, that Sherlaith kept giving me sidelong glances whilst her brother recounted tales of our Latin teacher and his mannerisms. Her tinkling laugh, like everything else about her, delighted me. I considered that the situation was precipitating. I was falling in love with my best friend's sister. I needed to take care, for I could not know how it might affect our friendship if I pursued the matter.

It was not an urgent problem because a gigantic auburn-haired and -bearded fellow with a sack slung over his muscular shoulder strode in!

"By Jayzuz!" he bellowed, "If that is not our Lu-i! Welcome, welcome, my boy!" His eye passed over to me, "And who is this blond-haired pirate?"

"Father!" Sherlaith protested, "Is that any way to speak of our guest?"

He guffawed; it must have been his way, laid the sack on a bench with a jangle, strode around the table and clasped my hand.

"Welcome to my home, stranger, for a stranger you'll remain until this *sea rat* of a son of mine introduces you!"

He bellowed with laughter again, a tear of mirth running down one cheek at the sight of Lugaid's outraged face. It was impossible not to warm to this larger-than-life figure, in every sense of the term, and I grinned up in his face. A bone-crushing squeeze of the hand and he released his grip.

"Father, this is my best friend, Aella, he's from Northumbria—"

"And he's the best leather-worker in that land, aren't you, Aella?" Sherlaith cut in.

I frowned at her, "Do you believe everything your brother says?"

She pouted, "When it suits me," she said lowering her head.

"Ale!" the master of the house roared and moments later the young woman came with a large jug brimming with foam and a drinking horn in her other hand. She served him first and then filled our beakers. Now it was my turn to be thoroughly questioned about my life and activities. The chieftain was too astute to take an unknown person into his household even temporarily. From his manner of eliciting information, I realised how his intelligence had helped re-establish an ancient family of Osraige on the throne. I would not wish to cross him in any way, so it was a relief when he thundered—he seemed incapable of speaking softly, "Any friend of Lugaid's is welcome in my home and a friend of mine!" he beamed and Sherlaith clapped her hands.

At that moment, I could think of nothing more pleasant than staying with his family.

FOURTEEN

THE FIRST FEW DAYS IN ARDFINNAN WILL REMAIN WITH me for the rest of my life even though those long blissful hours came to an abrupt end. They started well as I scrounged some hay and began to weave it into shape.

"Aella! What so occupies your mind that you have no thought for anything else?"

She meant any*one*, judging from her feigned petulant tone; but that was swiftly remedied as I wanted nothing more than Sherlaith's company.

"Will you not join me? For, see, I'm weaving a head."

"A *head!* What on earth for?"

I smirked and teased her,

"If you are patient, you'll see! But first, the neck...the throat is the most important part of all."

"You're not making the whole body, I hope, or else you'll need more straw. I'll go and fetch some." She leapt up eagerly from her brief perching next to me on a fallen tree trunk I'd chosen as a seat."

"Wait! This fine fellow doesn't need a body," I waved the head, complete with a neck at her. Before her arrival and my weaving, I had found and trimmed a long, slender branch, suitable for use as a pole, whose ends I had whittled to a point. I picked it up and, carrying it and the straw head, began to walk away from her, confident that curiosity would make her trail after me.

"Hey! Where do you think you're going?"

"Well away from any footpath."

She followed as I knew she would as I marched towards the edge of a cleared field. Just before reaching the boundary, I stopped to plant the branch into the ground, then positioned the straw head carefully on the upright point.

"Ah, I see!" she yipped, "A scarecrow! But that's no good, silly, without some old rags, I'll go and fetch some!"

"Wait! It's no scarecrow. This is a target."

She looked confused, perhaps wondering why I had come thus far without carrying a bow and arrows. Still, I wished to prolong her torment, so I said appreciatively, "Your legs are long enough, Ser-la. Will you kindly measure me twelve paces from the target?"

How could she refuse? When she'd done it, I whipped out my seax and marked the spot with a line in the earth. When I was satisfied, she looked at me balefully and I had to laugh at her expression.

"So, what will you aim at your target, now you've gone to all this trouble?"

"This!" I drew my throwing knife from my belt with a flourish and held the tip of the blade between finger and thumb."

"That!" she looked incredulous and wide-eyed at the weapon, but her disbelief reached new heights when I said,

"This is only useful if you strike the throat, killing your man."

"Impossible from here," she dismissed the idea with a disdainful sniff.

I placed the toe of my boot on the mark, turned slightly sideways, took aim and hurled the blade with deadly accuracy at the straw throat, which it penetrated unerringly.

Sherlaith gazed open-mouthed and chirruped,

"That was no fluke, was it? Can you do it again? I wish to study your technique."

"Willingly. But I must repair the straw—it's a sorry mess." I strode over, feeling pleased with myself for impressing this pretty young woman. A few deft twists of the straw and it was ready for my next throw. After years of practice, I was confident of hitting the spot anew. I toed the line and felt her narrowed eyes boring into me. Fast as an adder, I flung the knife and again struck the throat.

With a confident grin, I looked at her for acclamation or even adulation—but instead of praise, she said, witheringly,

"Anyone can do that with such a good knife."

I was hurt and astonished but without a word, strode to the target, pulled out the weapon, repaired the straw and hurried back to her. I passed the weapon, hilt-first, to her and said sardonically,

"Anyone, eh? Well, maybe I should draw a line five paces nearer?"

"Don't be so condescending! I'll hit it from where you did."

I had to admire her pluck but fully expected her to miss the straw completely so that I could laugh at her expense. However, she sidled up to the line, placed her foot exactly as I had done and took careful aim, with an outstretched arm, between knife and target. The blade flew straight and true but did not pierce the throat.

"Oh, well done, Ser-la!"

Her eyes flashed at me,

"Do not tease me or I'll use it on you!"

I rushed over to retrieve the weapon before she could get her hands on it.

"Look," I said, my hand still resting on the hilt, before removing the weapon, "You made a fair mess of the fellow's face, I'd say you struck between the teeth and the eye. It might well have been fatal! Nay, I'd not tease one such as *you*—first attempt and all," I ended up muttering. But she'd heard me and was grinning.

"I must have our smith make me a throwing knife!"

But I didn't think it would be so easy or such a good idea. I hoped she would never use a similar weapon in the heat of the moment. But I kept my thoughts to myself.

She gazed at me and smiled,

"It's a fine day, will you come down to the creek with me to help gather watercress?"

Anything for her company, but I worried where Lugaid might be and whether he was missing me. Without a trace of hesitation that might damage me in her eyes, I replied,

"I'd love to be of service and finding watercress is more useful than throwing knives."

Of course, I didn't mean that, but wished to ingratiate myself with my best friend's sister.

"As to usefulness, you'd not stop an enemy by hurling watercress at him, Aella."

I laughed but would not be bested,

"And you might have trouble chewing and swallowing a throwing knife gracing your salad!"

She giggled and linked her arm though mine,

"Is there not some forlorn maid waiting in Northumbria for your return?"

I clicked my tongue,

"Oh, ay, there's my old mother. Does that count?"

She laughed gaily, and pressed against my side,

"I confess, I had someone young and pretty in mind."

To put an end to this conversation, I decided to be abrupt.

"Nay, none such."

But I couldn't help but notice her self-satisfied smile. What was going on in that chestnut-crowned head of hers? Whatever it was became instantly dismissed at the sight of the creek running into the River Suir.

"You might need your knife to cut the cress, Aella."

"Wait here. I have my boots and I won't have you get your feet muddy."

She smiled and I think she blushed for the first time, but with pleasure.

"You do know what cress looks like, don't you?"

I straightened my shoulders and, without replying, looked offended and marched down to the stream.

I worked quickly and came back with a large bunch of cress, handing it over to her with a smug expression on my face.

She took it and carried it to her nose, sniffed and with a look of disgust flung the bundle to the grass and ground it down with her heel.

"What the...?

I gaped and she said,

"*Aella*, you are hopeless! That's water parsnip and it's poisonous; it smells of carrot, that's how to tell it from watercress! Never mind, I'll go—"

I clutched her arm, and looked imploringly at her,

"No, let me try again. If it smells of carrot, I'll leave it be."

I bent over to retrieve a sprig, both to sniff it – unmistakeably carroty – and for identification.

"Well, all right, just don't bring Fool's Watercress again, next time!"

I growled that I'd fetch the best cress in Ériu. Reappearing in several minutes, I handed her a second bunch, which must have been good, because she simply sniffed it and said,

"Well done!"

The next few days were similar. She had me picking both cooking and eating apples one day, pears another and onions and leeks on the morrow. Also, she showed me her favourite hideaway she used when she wanted to be alone and I knew then I was irretrievably lost to her charms.

This idyllic situation came to an end on the fifth day of my stay. I was outside in the courtyard chatting with Lugaid when a familiar cutting voice said,

"What's *he* doing here? As if seeing that face at Lismore isn't enough!"

Colum MacBroian! Expressing my precise sentiments on seeing *him*.

Lugaid stared hard at our classmate and his expression was not welcoming.

"Aella's my guest and you'll keep a civil tongue in your head if you've tramped all this way to see me."

The answer was swift and sharp,

"Don't flatter yourself, Lu-i, there are better reasons for tramping here."

And that was the first glimmer I had of his interest in Sherlaith. During the next few minutes, I learnt that he lived in the village with the market: Clogheen. In that short time, he was almost friendly until Sherlaith appeared.

"Lovely weather is it not, Mistress Ser-la?"

Sherlaith smiled, but at me not him, and affirmed that such a day it was. Quick-witted as ever, I spotted the fleeting contortion of his face. Jealousy!

Well this is a worrying turn of events!

The minx made matters worse.

"It *is* lovely weather, Colum MacBroian. In truth, I went down to the creek with Aella and he gathered cress for me. Now wasn't that a kindly act?"

The younger man flushed and muttered something not meant to be heard. Worse still, the maiden had not finished tormenting him.

"Would *you* like to walk out with me in that direction, Colum?"

My heart sank, but I knew she was up to no good by her tone. He noticed nothing untoward and eagerly accepted, offering her his arm and casting a triumphant sneer my way.

"Is that a knife at your belt, Colum?

"It is, indeed."

"And can you throw it?"

Now I knew what she was about, I almost, but not quite, felt sorry for him.

She laughed that tinkle of hers and they set off out of the yard.

Lugaid glanced at me.

"Do you know what she's about? I know that laugh, and it bodes ill."

"I made a target..." and I told him the whole tale, ending, "...she'll make him look a fool."

My friend set off at a run, "Come on then," he called over his shoulder, "we mustn't miss it for anything!"

By the time we reached the field, the two of them seemed to be arguing.

Colum was red in the face and started to shout.

"And I tell you, it's impossible. Nobody could hit that straw-man from *that* distance."

He glowered at her and was so aroused that he hadn't noticed us arriving.

She contrived a pitying expression,

"You certainly couldn't, it seems. Why don't you... try again? And if you put the point in its throat from there, I'll give you a kiss, upon my word I will."

He looked at her with desperate determination and held his knife between finger and thumb, but it was never designed for throwing and the effort, despite him putting all his might behind the throw, fell far short of the pole.

She laughed and, worse still, so did Lugaid, mortifying him, but I kept silent.

"There, I told you it couldn't be done!" Colum protested as red in the face as a Spanish radish.

"Oh, but it can! You can do it, can't you, Aella? Go on, same conditions!"

Something told me to walk away, but the promise of a kiss from those luscious lips blew good sense away like chaff on the wind. Instead, I stepped up to the mark, drew my knife, and in a swift action planted it in the throat of the straw dummy.

"Oh, Aella!" she skipped over to me and pressed a long, lingering—magnificent—kiss on my lips. I thought my heart would burst with happiness but feared that Colum's would rupture with rage. He stood glowering and speechless, walking silently a few paces behind us as we three returned to the hall.

Inside the building, Sherlaith sensibly found an excuse to slip away, but not before shooting flirtatious glances at me, to Colum's vexation. As soon as she'd left us, in a show of traditional Osraige hospitality, Lugaid called for beakers and ale and tried his best to cheer up our glum schoolmate. He said fairly,

"You couldn't expect to throw as well as Aella, he was once a warrior."

"Ay, true enough, and my knife is made for throwing. Yours is meant for other work, Colum."

The poor fellow looked grateful and if he had to hold a grudge against anyone, it should have been the maid but as the weeks ahead were to prove, he couldn't digest his resentment, aiming it squarely at me.

FIFTEEN

LISMORE ABBEY, MAY 686 AD

THE DAY OF MY DEPARTURE FROM THE UÁ BROÍTHE farmstead was the saddest of my life, other than that of the loss of Edwy. Saying my farewells to Sherlaith made it so. We were alone in a shady bower in the courtyard, its latticework covered in an early-blooming rambling rose. The dappled sunlight through the delicate pink petals and buds sought in vain to cheer our gloomy faces.

Sherlaith glanced into the yard and even though reassured we were not being overheard, as if not daring to give voice to her feelings, whispered in my ear,

"Aella, you have stolen my heart. Promise you will come for me when your studies are ended. I will wait for you."

My pulse skipped and beat faster at her words; it was true, then, she loved me as much as I adored her. But now I had to leave her to return to my tedious declinations. My mind raced. What should I say to her? I reached into my belt and drew out my throwing knife.

"Take this, Ser-la, it is my most precious possession. When I come to repossess it, I will take you along with it. Meanwhile,

practise every day until you never miss and when you do, think
of me."

Her voice thick with emotion, she said,

"Oh, Aella! Then our troth is plighted."

"It is my solemn pledge," I said, my joy uncontained.

Her lips sought mine and, for the first time, our kisses were
passionate and desperate.

"That's enough, you two!"

But there was a laugh in Lugaid's voice. Controlling his
mood, he put on a stern expression and directed it at me,

"How dare you, my guest, conduct yourself in this way?"

Sherlaith leapt up and waved my throwing knife under his
nose,

"Ach! Shut up, Lu-i! We are betrothed, aren't we, Aella?"

She stared defiantly at her brother, who gazed at me in
wonder.

"It is true," I said.

"And does Father know about this?" He looked crossly
at her.

She stamped her foot and her eyes flashed. "Not yet," she
said but lowered her defiant chin in confusion.

Lugaid stepped over to me and took me in an embrace to
whisper in my ear,

"Father likes you well enough; I shouldn't think he'll
object. But don't you think you should seek his consent?"

I clapped him on the back and we both ignored Sherlaith's
flashing eyes when she demanded,

"What did you say to Aella?"

"Men's business," he said and smirked.

As we walked away from her towards the hall, I murmured
to him,

"Watch your back, I gifted her my throwing knife."

He stared at me incredulously, "Then you must truly love Ser-la!"

His father was sitting by the hearth with a grey shaggy head resting adoringly on his knee whilst he thoughtlessly ran his fingers through the hound's fur. As we approached, its feathered tail thumped against the floor in greeting.

"Father, Aella wishes for a word with you."

"Ay, it's time for you to go, lads, I know. Well," he rose to tower over me and stuck out a huge hand. I felt intimidated and swallowed hard, "it's been a pleasure having you here, Aella. Come whenever you like."

"Thank you, sir. But I wished to speak with you on an important matter."

His bushy eyebrow raised.

"I seek your consent, sir, for my betrothal with Ser-la. She feels as I do."

There were many more things I wanted to add but my throat was so dry and I did not want it to waver and let me down. He looked at me from under bristling eyebrows and his expression was grim. But then again, I'd rarely seen it otherwise.

Suddenly, it relaxed into a smile.

"Run, Lugaid, fetch your sister, I wish to scold her!"

But I knew he was jesting because his eyes twinkled just like his daughter's when she was being impish. And he prolonged the silence to strain my nerves further until she arrived looking anxious, her brother two paces behind. Strangely, the hound whined as though it sensed the tension in his mistress.

"Well, here we are then," said the chieftain, "This is an *odd* business." We three looked uneasily at him. But he smiled, "Aella must be special. You have rejected all suitors, lassie, and the first Saxon to enter our door makes you lose your head. Do you know what they say hereabouts? Or have you forgotten? Wives and oxen are best found in one's own neighbourhood."

Sherlaith looked defiant, "But Father, this is not a question of a wife, but a husband."

"Same thing!" he said grumpily.

"And Aella *is* special!"

The chieftain guffawed and I felt offended, but he scratched his head and the twinkle returned. He directed his humorous gaze at me.

"You do realise what a wildcat you'll be taking off my hands?"

"I have some idea, sir." I grinned because this was a kind of acceptance.

"Well, rather you than me!"

"Oh, Father!" she flung herself at him and smothered him in kisses, then pushed him away and glared, her tone was abrasive, "What do you mean by *that*, exactly?"

I missed the exchange because Lugaid was embracing me and calling me *"brother"*.

Betrothal delayed our departure for Lismore since Sherlaith's father insisted on a feast and much drinking to celebrate. He ordered two of the cattle to be slaughtered for roasting and sent men out throughout the area with messages. The next day, the hall was crammed to bursting with members of the *tuath* and my back was slapped and health drunk countless times. Seeing the torrents of ale consumed, I dreaded to think what the wedding feast itself would be like, and sloughed away into a deep gloom at the thought of having to finish my studies first.

Our march back to the abbey was full of lively chatter and the early May countryside appeared more lovely than ever to my besotted eyes. I told Lugaid that I intended to study like a man possessed so that I could bring forward my discharge with a judgement as proficient. On that carefree journey, little could I suspect that events would conspire to keep we lovers apart for far longer than I hoped.

The abbot summoned me to his quarters upon my return. My talent with the quill was my undoing. In my absence, the abbot had spoken about my calligraphic abilities to the prior in charge of the scriptorium. The latter, desperate for help in the timely completion of a volume, had implored for my release from afternoon classes to lend a hand with this project.

"But Father Abbot," I pleaded to no avail, "that will delay my achieving proficiency in Latin reading. It will at least double the time before I return to Northumbria." I made no mention of my betrothal.

"My son, we must all respond present at God's calling. You will obey my order."

That was the end of the matter, but hidden within it was a priceless jewel of an opportunity, which I could not at that stage suspect.

The months slipped by until autumn mists shrouded the valley below the abbey and the grey figures seen through a veil resembled ghosts, even yet going about their daily business. Up to that period, I maintained my promise, or boast, to Lugaid and took my Latin to a new level but Brother Senach was not a teacher to waste words on praise. I knew my worth as a student since I was quickest to answer his questions. I hoped that the end of the year report would bring my emancipation.

Meanwhile, in the scriptorium, something fundamental to my future happened. In the first place, despite my reluctance to go there, the advancing weeks saw me develop a firm friendship with Prior Brian. I believe he appreciated hard workers of few words, and a casual event occurred to cement the sentiment. One day, one of the older monks was stricken by such bad back pain that he could not sit at his desk. The prior bemoaned his lot,

"What are we to do brothers? We are all busy with our different tasks, but this most experienced of our brethren was preparing the initial for the first line of the Gospel. The volume cannot leave these walls without it."

I stepped over to peer at the parchment. The old monk had outlined the top of the initial *I* ready for colouring, but in my mind's eye, the elaborate tail of the letter was still to be committed to the yellow-white surface.

"Father Prior, if you are willing, this is something I can do."

Monks are not given to sneering at their fellows, but I am certain that two or three of my fellow scribes lapsed into smirks.

"What makes you think you can do this, Aella? You, who have no experience of lettering?"

"Father, it is not so dissimilar to the curvilinear work"—I said this in Latin to impress them all— "I used to inscribe on leather."

The prior overcame what qualms he might have had and I began to sketch the tail of the initial from memory of my mother's brooch. Occasionally, he came over to grunt his approbation before returning to his work. True, I had no experience of laying on the colours but I tried to use good sense and worked out a scheme of my own. First, I outlined in gold; once this was done, I painted the pale tints and left them to dry whilst I returned to my desk and wrote some more lines; then, I used a darker shade of the same hue for shadowing, to create an illusion of depth. I had noticed nobody had done this in the previous work and it was something I brought from my leather-working experience. I leaned back and considered my effort; pleased, I added some light touches of white and a few strokes of gold to the interior design of the initial.

"The Lord be Praised!" Prior Brian exclaimed. "The initial seems to spring off the page. Aella, an angel has guided your hand."

I wanted to tell him that the effect was created by the shadowing, but who was to say that an angel had not inspired my idea? So, I kept silent and beamed. This was a one-off occasion, but it would prove important in my future.

The end of year report was a matter of weeks away, but then the second event of consequence occurred. Before Latin class, one morning, Lugaid hurried over to me in great agitation.

"Have you heard?"

It was unlike him to lose his calm, he was more given to pranks, so I supposed this to be just another jest. Diffidently, I smiled at him,

"Think not to outwit me, my friend, for I have the besting of you!"

He looked stricken and I began to suspect something was amiss.

"Nay, Aella, this is no hoax: it is war! The abbey is compelled to fight to right a grave injustice."

"The abbey fight... and with whom?"

"With the monastery of Kilcrumper which lies four leagues to the west in the Kingdom of Munster."

"That cannot be, abbeys and monasteries do not fight each other."

"What world do you live in, Aella? Throughout the land, they often resort to force to settle disputes. Why else do you think Lismore has defensive ramparts on the townward side? For what other reason does the abbot maintain a band of men at arms?"

I'd never given it a thought, but it made sense.

"What is the dispute about?"

"The usual things: territory and cattle. The monks of Kilcrumper slew three herdsmen and made off with their beasts. Not content, they claim falsely that Lismore was abusing *their* pastureland. Father Abbot checked the deeds and Lismore holds those lands. He called on my father to gather men to fight and he is raising the tuath. So, you see, I have to go and fight beside him."

"I'll come with you!" I said on impulse, but I'll need an axe and a shield."

We hastened to take our leave of Brother Senach, who seemed to take hostilities between religious houses as a matter of course and contented himself with a blessing. Thence, we joined the abbot's warriors who were preparing to depart to unite with the Uá Broíthe tuath. A friendly grin from me to Calum, who had joined us carrying a short stabbing spear, elicited an unfriendly glower. I shrugged and blamed it on pre-battle nerves. I spoke to the leader of the abbey force and soon had a stout shield on my arm and an axe strapped on my back. It was not as comfortable to wield as mine, but I had no doubt I would make it sing a blood song.

SIXTEEN

KILCRUMPER, OCTOBER 868 AD

THERE WAS NO QUESTION OF FORMING A SHIELD-WALL since the Irish like the Picts, fought on the run. First, came a hail of missiles and then the charging together for hand to hand combat. To ward off the projectiles, I held my shield covering my face and head. This was a wise precaution because I had to use my axe to hack off a shaft deeply embedded in the linden wood. This had to be done quickly as the foe was on the charge, but the arrow made the shield unbalanced and unwieldy.

The recollection of battle incidents is generally fleeting and incoherent in my experience, but two things stand out from that fray: I saved Lugaid's life and he delivered mine. He was assailed by two enemies at the same time and, since I had just dispatched my ferocious adversary, I was able to spin and deal a shuddering axe blow to the nearest of them, who was on the point of ramming a short spear into my friend's exposed chest. Thanks to my intervention, that did not happen. I was in time to regain my stance and parry a sword thrust with my shield from another fierce foe. My weapon bit deep into his collar bone and he collapsed at my feet, where I finished him.

As I straightened, Lugaid paid off his battle debt to me. Oddly, the blow came from behind, a glancing strike under the left shoulder. It knocked me to the ground and, in a blind panic, since a man is vulnerable on his knees amidst the enemy, I struggled to my feet but could not raise my shield. The pain below the collar bone was too great. I had to let my wooden protector slip to the grass and rely on fighting one-handed with my axe swinging wildly, my left arm hanging limply by my side. I swore under my breath: if only I'd brought my leather armour with me here in Ériu. As it was, like Lugaid, I was wearing my everyday clothes.

I stared around me, but the enemy was either lying dead or gravely wounded on the ground or gone. Gazing at the carnage on the ground around me, I saw Colum MacBroian's body. A pang of sorrow stabbed me but then I took in Lugaid's grinning face and I frowned, also at the realisation that apart from the dead and wounded we were alone. I raised my eyes and stared in the distance, where our men were pursuing the routed survivors.

"Colum is dead," I stated the obvious.

"Ay, do you care, man?"

Something in my friend's tone was amiss, so I scrutinised his face. I was about to say that I supposed I did care when Lugaid said,

"The coward got what he deserved."

"What do you mean?"

"*I* killed him."

I gazed thunderstruck at this affirmation but could not absorb it.

"You slew Colum! But why?" It made no sense—he had fought on our side.

"Ay, the villain went for you, Aella. I wasn't going to let him slay my *brother*. So, I managed to strike him down barely in time. As it was, I deflected the force of the blow, hence your slight wound. But it will need washing, lest infection sets in."

We began to tramp after our victorious warriors towards the monastery in the distance. But I didn't care about the stinging wound; I was trying to understand.

"But why? Why would Colum wish to harm me?"

Lugaid levelled me a pitying stare,

"What, have you no idea, Aella?"

"None."

Frowning and as if talking to himself, said, "Colum always wooed Ser-la but she never cared for him. Also, he didn't come to the betrothal feast." He raised his voice from little more than a mutter, "Did you notice he didn't come? He will have heard about it though, from his family. The father drank your health, Aella, whilst the son sought to skewer you!"

"Colum must have been consumed by bitterness, but it was a wretched thing to do. We could have fought face to face."

"Except that he knew you were the better warrior. He hoped his treachery would go unseen on the battlefield, but he reckoned without us covering for one another. More than ever, we're brothers, brother!" he chortled.

"Ay, that we are!" I said, flinging my good arm over his shoulder.

Before long, we heard the unmistakeable screams of the wounded in the throes of mortal combat. Another fifty paces and we came in sight of the monastery. Even as we approached, our men were banging weapons on their shields and calling for the abbot to emerge. Lugaid explained that there was a convention to be followed. No harm would come to the abbot or his monastery but we had gained the right of redress. In short, we were admitted into the courtyard and agreement for the restitution of our beasts and an indemnity for the deaths was reached—not of our warriors, for that was considered an act of God, but of the three herdsmen, for that was held to be a crime. A sum was settled and paid and an oath sworn henceforth to leave Lismore territory unviolated— altogether a satisfactory outcome. As soon as this was concluded, Lugaid left the side of his father, where together they had overseen the settlement, to re-join me.

"Come, follow me!"

I did so without question, which proved to be an excellent decision. The infirmarian was a skilled healer and bathing away the dried blood pinning my tunic to the wound, he washed it thoroughly with vinegar, which stung like devil's spittle! Then, he smoothed an ointment over the wound and bound it with clean linen.

"Naught will go amiss with yon wound, son." I noticed he addressed Lugaid even if it was *my* wound. "But after two days, remove the cloth, gently rinse the wound and pat it dry, then smooth more of this balm over the cut and repeat the procedure at least twice, by which time it will be on the mend."

I left the infirmarian two silver sceattas for the monastery coffers, much to Lugaid's disgust. For him, Kilcrumper Monastery had forsaken all rights of friendship for perpetuity. Weariness overcame me and the thought of the four-league march stretching ahead of us did not appeal. Not knowing the land hereabouts, I explained how the battle and loss of blood had weakened me, so asked my friend,

"How far is it from here to Ardfinnan?"

Lugaid guffawed and all of a sudden, his face grew serious,

"Surely, you don't want Ser-la fussing over your scratch! Besides, it's four leagues to the abbey and six to my home."

I groaned, moaning, "I can't manage either right now, I just want to lie down."

"And so, you shall! Come with me. I explored this land in my youth and know the very place."

After what seemed to have been an age, he brought me to a low wooden structure with a turf roof. A cow byre stood sheltered and inviting, luckily without beasts in residence.

"Lend me your seax, a moment."

I drew the blade and handed it to Lugaid. He went off a few paces and began to scythe at ferns that were beginning to change from green to gold. He gathered a large bundle of bracken and disappeared into the byre. Returning, he collected an equal quantity and disappeared indoors again.

"Come on then," he called and I ducked into the dim interior. "There!" He pointed proudly at his handiwork. A feeding trough on a trestle was lined with ferns and a more inviting mattress had I rarely seen. I sat on the edge of the manger and swung my legs inside, whilst he helped me get my shoulders down flat. "I'll go and fetch myself some bracken to cover the floor," he said brightly as if he hadn't fought as hard as anyone among us.

When he'd closed the rickety door and settled beside the wall, I said,

"It wouldn't take a bull much effort to batter down that door."

He laughed and said, "Listen, brother, if that is all you can think about now you are lying in luxury whilst I suffer, you must do penance."

"And what might that be?"

"You can translate your idle thought into Latin!"

He thought I wouldn't be able to do it, and I let him think so before attempting it,

"Quod non multum accipies de armento forisque pariter refringi conatus est ianuam."

There was no way he could spot a mistake, only Brother

Senach, our venerable magister could do that. Nonetheless, Lugaid snorted and hazarded, "I'll wager that's wrong!"

I reckoned it probably was and lay there for a while working on it, resolving to memorise my effort to check with Senach. I strained to listen to a rustling in the undergrowth near the wall and felt insecure but, supposing it to be nothing more dangerous than a fox, closed my eyes. Soon, despite Lugaid's snores, I, too, fell into a deep sleep.

"Aargh!" He woke me at dawn, with this cry, as he batted a rat off his thigh. There followed a string of oaths, interspersed with something along the lines of: "As well it didn't scrabble over my face!" This was a sentiment I heartily approved of, as I wouldn't rightly care for a rat scratching around in my beard, either.

Once awake, there seemed little point in delaying our departure, especially as the abbey offered the promise of sustenance. Neither of us had eaten or drunk since before the battle and this yearning, if anything, gave us added determination to cover the miles. We refreshed ourselves at a babbling stream we chanced upon, which helped, but it was well after noon when we entered the abbey courtyard. Welcomed back as if we'd been given up for lost, I smirked at the thought, for if we'd been among the fallen and risen up, superstition would have had the monks fleeing in all directions. A rapid explanation of our hunger and my wound weakness gained us a hot eel soup—one of my favourite meals, made better by chunks of bread fresh from the oven. Well-deserved, the rubicund cook told us, for had we not salvaged his cows from the miscreant monks of Kilcrumper?

This was, indeed so, and Lismore Abbey had added further martial experience to my grounding in reading, writing, and Latin, but my greatest Irish acquisition would, I hoped, even now be practising her knife-throwing skills in a meadow near Ardfinnan.

SEVENTEEN

LISMORE ABBEY AUTUMN AND WINTER 686-7 AD

A FEW DAYS AFTER OUR TRIUMPHANT RETURN, I MET with defeat. The end of year reporting had been delayed owing to the situation at Kilcrumper but as abbey life returned to normal, a summons arrived. My encounter with Abbot Mo-Chuaróc began cheerfully when he praised me for my excellent contribution to the scriptorium and the war. Since he was in an amiable mood, he proceeded by saying,

"It makes me wonder, my son, whether your calling that we oft-times discussed may involve your talent with the quill and the brush. You have all the skills to make a complete book from the covers to the contents—it's quite remarkable!" He chuckled, amused at his discerning observation.

For my part, there and then, I barely gave it a thought, being far more occupied with thoughts about my progress in Latin. Nonetheless, I frowned and thought that if God wanted me to produce a book, He would surely specify which volume He wanted. I pushed the matter aside, unaware that the abbot had planted a seed destined to germinate and fructify.

Suddenly, the venerable monk spoke to me rapidly in

Latin. I suppose either he wanted to trip me up or make me feel inadequate, for the gist was that my Latin was not yet deemed proficient.

"But Father Abbot, I have been diligent and keep up my studies, I answer all Brother Senach's questions more readily than my classmates!"

Reacting to my tone, he said,

"Even so, Aella, I am guided by Brother Senach, who is adamant that you are still not proficient in Latin. There is the reputation of the abbey to consider. I was expressly tasked to ensure your level was at the highest possible standard—"

"But—"

His piercing eyes flashed, "I *will* finish. Therefore, you will remain under Senach's tutelage until he is satisfied. Only then will I review your situation. Meanwhile," at this point he smiled benignly, "however reluctantly, I am relieving you of all duties in the scriptorium so that you may concentrate on your language learning. Now, send in Lugaid Uá Broíthe."

There was no use arguing, "Thank you, Father Abbot," I bowed, grinding my teeth, and left his quarters. Lugaid was waiting in the corridor, "Your turn," I said curtly and continued to walk past him, but he caught my arm and hauled me to a halt.

"What's the matter, Aella?"

"Brother Senach has his misgivings. I am to remain."

Lugaid's face lit up and I felt churlish that I had wanted to leave him alone to his fate,

"Thank goodness, brother, I felt sure I was going to lose you."

"Don't you see, this means I can't marry Sherlaith and I'll have to listen to old Senach chuntering on for another *whole* year. Anyway, you'd better not keep the Abbot waiting."

I said this because I didn't want to hear any words of

consolation. I was inconsolable. All my waking hours outside of the classroom were spent recalling her beautiful twinkling eyes and my nights were devoted to dreaming about her soft lips. I thought I might go mad and wanted to wring the elderly magister's neck. But I was too wily to show him my true feelings, and buckling down to Latin syntax was the only way to gain the longed-for discharge from the abbey. The sooner I achieved that, the sooner I would marry Sherlaith.

I had hoped that the great feast of Christ's Mass might be spent away from the monastery and in my betrothed's arms. No such luck—it was the festival dearest to Abbot Mo-Chuaróc's heart. I came to love it, too; especially the two fine songs for the Nativity: *Jesus Refulsit Omnium,* which, as I told that slacker Lugaid, meant 'Jesus, Light of All the Nations'. Brother Senach informed us that it was written by Saint Hilary of Poitiers more than two hundred years before. Instead, I preferred singing lustily to *Corde natus ex Parentis,* the Abbot's favourite, 'Of the Father's Love Begotten', who told me that this was penned in the Roman province of Tarraconensis—not that I had the faintest idea of where that was—by a certain Aurelius Prudentius Clemens, about the same time as Saint Hilary's song.

Christ's Mass was the occasion I needed to lift me out of my despondency. I especially enjoyed the monks' re-enactment of the Nativity. It was a wonder to behold: the brothers built a stable with a manger in the courtyard. They brought an ox and a donkey and to my vexation, chose Lugaid to act the role of Saint Joseph, for which they provided him with a false white beard. Wouldn't Brother Senach, with his real white hair have made the perfect Joseph? To my frustration, a very pretty maid from the town was dressed as Mary to recite opposite my friend. Somehow, they obtained a little babe to be Our Saviour. I thought it as well that they swaddled him tightly against the chilly Lismore air. All in all, it was a marvellous occasion, enjoyed by the brothers and the townsfolk, who gasped in wonder at the performance. More than ever, they realised that God had sent His son among them for their salvation. How I howled with laughter when some of them ran away in terror when the Angel Gabriel appeared! Did the superstitious fools believe that Brother Fiach had truly descended from heaven?

So, the feast of Christ's Mass passed in joyous fraternity and the generous gift-giving of the monks to the poor of the town. My problems slipped away in this atmosphere and the arrival of the New Year brought the promise of my eventual release from study. I considered every day a step forward and one on which I could improve my Latin; otherwise, I feared I would grow old within those walls. Instead, a messenger came to Lismore, bearing devastating news.

The abbot sent for me one day towards the end of March.

"I have sorrowful tidings, Aella, on the twentieth day of March our brother in Christ, the Blessed Cuthbert, was taken to Our Lord's bosom."

"Why? He was not so old!"

My reaction was a kind of rebuttal and, unusually for me, I felt tears pricking at my eyes.

"Be not too sad, my son, you know that your friend will be in heaven among the angels."

I went away and thought deeply about everything I could remember of him; about every word he had told me. I think that day, the seedling the abbot had planted in my mind began to stir. In the immediate present, I thought about the details the elderly monk had provided me through the messenger from Lindisfarena: Cuthbert had spent his last days alone and in great pain on one of the inner Farne Isles with only seabirds for company. Alas! I had not been there to succour him, trapped as I was in an Irish monastery. My two oldest friends were gone—

praise God that in exchange He had given me Lugaid and as a consequence Sherlaith!

The demise of Cuthbert would have consequences for me, enabling the fulfilment of my dearest wish. Thus, even in death, Cuthbert was a true friend to me. But let me not get ahead of myself. The abbot in his wisdom sent a report of my progress to King Aldfrith and he had mentioned not only my Latin: it later transpired that this played an important role in Aldfrith's summons. The document arrived with another messenger in April when green buds were swelling in the monks' orchard.

The call to Abbot Mo-Chuaróc's quarters came as a complete surprise. His soulful and friendly gaze had me searching for meaning, but his words soon made it clear.

"It seems we are to lose you, Aella," my heart leapt, "for King Aldfrith, satisfied with our report, has requested your immediate return to Lindisfarena. Brother Senach assures me that you have made strides with your studies, for which I commend you. My son, carry forth with honour the name of Lismore and take with you my deepest gratitude for your contribution to our poor house."

"Father Abbot, I trust you will favour me with your presence at my forthcoming wedding."

He looked shocked and then thoughtful.

"My dear son, I had no idea you were betrothed, but it explains why you were so eager to leave the bosom of the abbey: another bosom allures you!" He chortled heartily at his daring jest. Then, he added, regretfully, "I fear the journey to Northumbria will be too demanding for these old bones. Will you pardon an old man's frailty?"

I beamed at him, "It is no Northumbrian maid, Father, but Sherlaith Uá Broíthe. Her home is but four leagues hence, as you well know. It is my intention to wed in May and then with all haste obey King Aldfrith's summons."

The elderly abbot agreed unhesitatingly to attend the celebrations and accorded leave of absence also to Lugaid for the festivities. However, my friend had to remain in the abbey at his studies until two days before the wedding.

I left the place with scarcely a backward glance and with almost unseemly haste but remembered to say my farewells to certain chosen monks whom I considered friends, including the old magister, whose warm salutations favourably surprised me. The gifts of a skilled teacher, like Senach, are blessings we carry with us throughout our lives.

I had given no forewarning of my arrival in Ardfinnan, which to my mind made my apparition more exciting. Sneaking unnoticed into the Uá Broíthe courtyard was nigh on impossible thanks to the free-ranging geese and the somnolent hounds, both by instinct inclined to create a strident din whenever a stranger set foot in there. The cacophony alerted Sherlaith, who was carrying a pail of water from the pump when I triggered off the racket.

"Aella!" She put down the pail and flew into my arms.

"I have come for my knife."

Her lips sought mine and, breathless, we entered her father's hall. He was sitting by the hearth, using a whetstone to hone his sword blade.

"Where's Lugaid?" was his uncouth greeting.

"The monks will let him come two days before our wedding."

"Oh, ay, and when might that be?"

His eyes were twinkling again in that craggy, whiskery foreboding countenance.

I swallowed hard, "I had thought, in this forthcoming month of May."

A little cry escaped Sherlaith's throat.

"We will not! *'Wed in May and rue the day!'*" she recited.

I looked stricken, knowing I could not delay until June. There was Aldfrith's command to obey. I told them so.

"I can see no difficulty," said the chieftain, "we can soon sort the *dál*—"

"*Dál?*"

"Ach, you Saxons know nothing! The contract. You'll be wanting your dues for taking her off my hands!"

"Father!" she glared, but the familiar twinkle lit her eyes.

His brow furrowed in concentration and he began his calculations of land and cattle. The time had come for me to be forthright.

"Sir, my king has summoned me and I must return to Northumbria. I hope to come back to live here, but I must obey him and visit my parents. I know not whether my father will leave the place of his birth.

"You tell him there's a warm welcome here and as much call for a skilled leather-worker as in Northumbria."

"Ser-la, you will have to wait for me again. I beg your forbearance."

"Father, when can we organise the *comchengal?*"

"The *what?*"

They both laughed, "The *lánamanda!*" he roared with mirth.

She joined in, giggling, and said, "Or *núachrad.*"

I looked unhappy and they took pity. The chieftain said, "They are all our terms for wedlock and legal contract, Aella. Don't worry, you shall have the wench!"

"Father!"

He smirked and winked at me, "I see no reason why the feast can't be held three days from now. As to the contract, you'll take what I offer, I suppose?"

"That I will!" I wanted his daughter, not his lands.

"Well then, it's settled, I'll send out word. Three days hence it will be!"

"But I'll *not* wait for your return, Aella." Sherlaith delivered her axe blow and my heart sank. She squeezed my hand. "Don't look so glum. I'm coming with you to Northumbria: I've never been overseas."

Her father chortled, "At last! Peace in the farmstead! But seriously, Aella, see if you can come back with your folks; they'll want for nought here."

Sherlaith was quite happy for the *núachrad* to be the traditional hand-binding ceremony, but I wanted a priest to conduct a Church wedding. The next day, acting on her advice, I set off for Clonmel, three leagues to the east, since Sherlaith insisted there was a church there dedicated to Saint Mary.

I found the priest, a young fellow, who had been a monk at Lismore Abbey before taking holy orders, so we had something in common. Father Guaire, his name, agreed to return with me to Ardfinnan, where together we would build, and he would consecrate a temporary altar.

If the betrothal had been an occasion of heavy drinking and overeating, then our wedding eclipsed it, as the wild revelling continued into the next day. As tradition required, Sherlaith and I retired after the meal, before I drank too much, to consummate our marriage. I had very little experience of womankind and she none of men, but to say we managed would be an understatement. The thrill of lovemaking between a couple deeply in love cannot be surpassed on this earth. Exhausted and radiant we reappeared among the guests to the good-natured ribald banter of Sherlaith's *tuath*, and *mine* now, I supposed.

One more day and we bade farewell to her family; her

father had commandeered a boatman to take us in his curragh from the nearby stretch of the Avonmore to its mouth at the port of Youghal, where I'd arrived with the abbot, seemingly a lifetime ago. Amid the bustle of traders, I found a seafarer who directed us to a vessel due to sail for Northumbria. Its owner, a swarthy fellow with a roguish eye, who I did not take to, nonetheless agreed to give us passage for a fair price. My elation mounted at the thought of presenting Sherlaith to my parents and showing her my native land.

It was the last day of April and the mild, calm weather made the crossing bearable for my wife. Her excitement at mistaking the Isle of Man for Northumbria caused me much merriment. Once past the Isle, I knew that within two hours we would be ashore. I used another jealously-guarded silver ingot to buy a sturdy horse and lifted Sherlaith to sit in front of me, setting the beast a gentle pace across the country. We took lodgings at an inn overnight, as I feared travelling in the dark, and the poor creature needed to feed, drink and rest.

We approached Riding on the Corbridge road, where I stopped at Edwy's Cross and explained its story to Sherlaith. When I'd pointed out every detail of the carving and the bole on the nearby oak tree where once I'd sat, I said,

"Now we will go to my home, but on the morrow, I must away to Lindisfarena."

I was experiencing very mixed emotions. Part of me was afraid of what I would find. I had received no news from my parents for almost three years. Were they well? How would they receive my foreign bride? For the rest, I was excited.

I need not have worried. As we approached our house—after Sherlaith's it seemed small—I saw my father emerge from the workshop with an unfinished shoe in his hand. I knew he was about to inspect his stitching for any imperfection in the brighter outdoor light. But he heard the hoofbeat of our mount and raised his head with a startled expression.

"Aella! Can it be you, son?"

"Whoa!" I reined in the willing beast and leapt nimbly down, reaching up for Sherlaith to fall into my arms. I pushed her forward to encounter him.

"Meet your daughter, Oswin."

He scrutinised her face and I could tell he liked what he saw…even more so as she moved closer to embrace him. "Father, my name is Ser-la," and she kissed his cheek.

My mother burst out of the house and to my joy, she looked as well as her husband and no older than when I'd gone away.

"My, an' you're a bonny 'un!" she grinned at Sherlaith. They embraced and she asked, "How long have you been wed?"

"But these three days past. We came straight here from Ériu." Sherlaith said.

My mother and father exchanged glances, "Newly-weds!" he declared, "Then we must celebrate!"

He organised a feast, but not on so grand a scale as the Uá Broíthe festivities. Still, it gave me the chance to renew old acquaintances and present friends to Sherlaith, especially Nerian, who had a special place in my affections. He was now the miller in his own right, since, as I was saddened to learn his father had died a twelvemonth before.

At the dining table, eating and quaffing to our hearts' content, once more I experienced mixed feelings: on the one hand, I was relaxed and happy among old friends with my bride; on the other, I knew this contentment must end on the morrow when I would be at the mercy of a king's slightest whim.

EIGHTEEN

LINDISFARENA, MID-MAY 687 AD

"...AELLA, THE LEATHER-WORKER, FATHER ABBOT."

"Ay, I was told to expect you, my son. This is what you must do..."

So, at last, he revealed the mystery of why I'd been ordered to appear in Lindisfarena and not in Babbanburgh, directly before the king.

Remarkably, Aldfrith's orders, as delivered through the abbot, coincided with an impulse of mine, germinating ever since the Abbot of Lismore had planted a seed in my unconscious mind. On my journey to Northumbria, the persistent thought that nobody more than I had enjoyed the confidence of that saintly man, Cuthbert, blossomed into a decision to produce the *Vita Sancti Cuthberti*: the true account of my friend's life as spoken by him to me.

The king had ordered me to Lindisfarena based on the glowing reports received from Lismore and the knowledge of my privileged relationship with the saint. Having admired the cover of the Gospel of Saint John, which the abbot assured me was safely sealed in Cuthbert's coffin—a matter of pride and joy to me—King Aldfrith believed I could produce a similarly worthy tome about Cuthbert for him. The king intended not simply the binding, but the whole work, written and illustrated by my hand.

Why then this insistence on my arrival on the isle? The abbot explained:

"While our lord the king has great confidence in your skills, my son, he believes that you should first consult the volumes in our possession here on Lindisfarena. It is a question of presentation. The Abbey Chapter will not allow the transfer of our priceless manuscripts to Babbanburgh. In any case, here in the scriptorium, everything you require for the *opus* will be made available. Come with me to the library and I will show you the books the king wishes you to consult."

The volume he took lovingly from a shelf and laid on a lectern had a miserable worm-eaten leather cover and I vowed to replace it as soon as I had time, never suspecting that my time would become so priceless.

"It is old and delicate, my son, I recommend care with its pages. There are few copies in the world and the marvel lies in who penned it: none less than the sainted Holy Father, Gregory the Great, wrote the *Dialogi!* You should read it from cover to cover, paying particular attention to the style and form of the presentation. Approaching the task in true humility, you will learn much; careful reading cannot be rushed, but when eventually, you have finished and taken your notes, you may then accede to the *Vita Sancti Martini*, which is here."

I studied the second volume, curious as to why the learned abbot should consider the *Dialogi* more pertinent than a tome written specifically for the same purposes as the one I had in mind. Left alone with these treasures, I caressed the pages of the book about Saint Martin and gazed with wonder at the illustration of the soldier-saint slicing through his cloak to offer half to a shivering beggar. Ideas for illustrations about Cuthbert were already forming in my mind, but first, as Sulpicius Severus had done on Martin, I would have to commit the saint's life to a text.

Deciding not to begin reading at once, I made my way to the abbey crypt. The day after his death, Cuthbert's mortal remains were transferred there and already, drawn by the fame of his sanctity, pilgrims crossed daily to the isle to pray at his shrine.

Kneeling before the simple stone tomb, my prayer consisted of an apology for my absence at the time of his illness and passing. Unflinching and manly in battle, my emotions betrayed me before my friend's tomb, tears rolling silently down my cheeks, which I wiped angrily and roughly away with my sleeve. In that candlelit chamber, the growing certainty overwhelmed me that I must honour his life with my testimony.

Only when I emerged to breathe the outdoor air and gaze towards the coast of Northumbria did it occur to me how great a task I was about to shoulder and how little I'd see of my new bride. It would be inappropriate to bring Sherlaith to live among the monks, she'd be far better off living with my parents. For the foreseeable future, there was no question of returning to my wife's farmstead in Ériu or transferring my folks there.

Counterbalancing those regrets, was my ardent desire to set about the creation of the opus. It also occurred to me that apart from the reading suggested to me and recollections of my conversations with Cuthbert, there was a third avenue: there were people on the isle who had known him and could share their memories. In the forthcoming weeks and months, I would seek them out and commit their reminiscences to parchment.

My ideas crystallising into a plan of campaign, I returned to the abbey library to begin reading. Only a few lines into

Gregory's *Introduction*, a sense of my unworthiness for the task ahead submerged me. The pope-saint's words seemed to leap at me from the page: '*...my sorrow is increased, by remembering thrives of certain notable men, who with their whole soul did utterly forsake and abandon this wicked world: whose high perfection when I behold, I cannot also but see mine own infirmities and imperfection...*' Good heavens! If one such as he, honoured and given the appellation '*the Great*' by the Church, should feel inadequate in the face of the task, what hope was there for me?

I sighed and redoubled my concentration. It soon became clear that the formulation of the *Dialogues,* as the name suggested, consisted of exchanges between the great pope and his faithful deacon, Peter. In these, the Holy Father outlined episodes from the lives of saintly men, often referring to their deeds and miracles performed. He chose some unlikely personages: a gardener-monk, whose capture and treatment of a thief stealing his worts amused me. I began to see why the Abbot of Lindisfarena had chosen this volume as an example to follow.

Scribbling notes as I studied the pope's erudite writings, I worked until daylight faded, by then having reached the end of Chapter Five, about Constantinius, the virtuous clerk of the Church of St Stephen. My eyes were too tired to continue by candlelight and, pressingly, I had to make practical arrangements in the abbey for my stay.

To my surprise and pleasure, I found that the abbot had given predispositions for my meals and sleeping, so my bodily needs were not problematical, but worrying about whether I would cope with the king's commission troubled me. Pope Gregory's brilliant mastery of language and content, instead of inspiring me, had filled me with a sense of inadequacy. This state of mind deprived me of sleep and the more I lay awake, the more I missed Sherlaith. That first night, the prospect of endless years of suffering and toil hung over me like an incubus. Strange how uncompleted tasks awaiting attention rear up before one like mountains when, in reality, they are little more than knolls to be surmounted.

Already, a committed second day's reading led me to complete the notes on the twelfth and last chapter of the *Dialogues*. I sat back, chuckling about the priest who preferred to finish pruning his vines instead of hurrying to give the last rites to a dying man. It took a miracle to solve that situation, and maybe I would need one to write my book for King Aldfrith.

Carefully closing the tome, I examined the poor state of its binding and again promised to remedy its condition, but this would mean taking the volume to our workshop in Riding. Thought of home brought anguished images of Sherlaith. I wondered how many days must pass before I could honestly justify a break at home. The three I had spent so far were but a mere beginning, as became painfully clear when the abbot came to the library to check on my progress.

"I have finished the *Dialogues*, Father Abbot."

He looked at me askance, "How is that possible, my son? Have you already completed the pope's account of the life of Benedict of Nursia?"

I gaped at him and came down to earth with a bump.

"B-but I finished Chapter Twelve about the priest and his vines."

The abbot, a kindly soul, laughed and rested an arm around my shoulder, "That is Book One, Aella, the next volume, look, up there, next to it, is about Saint Benedict and *that* is the model you should follow for Cuthbert."

I didn't let him see me grind my teeth, but he knew I was feeling foolish and tried to alleviate my vexation.

"Our library is a whole new universe to explore, Aella, but fear not, you will soon be master of the material that serves for your undertaking."

"When I am ready to return to my home for a break, Father Abbot, I wish to take these two volumes with me. See how the bindings are reduced so shabbily. I would provide new ones worthy of the contents."

He looked troubled and I realised at once what books meant to the old man and how he would not bear to part with them. The monks spoke well of this Abbot Eadberht as one who favoured poverty, solitude and devotion. I, too, had only positive experiences of the man, who treated me kindly, and I could easily imagine him alone buried deep in the contents of a book. Now, he hurried away as if it was the best way of avoiding such an unpleasant thought as relinquishing books.

I sighed, took down the second volume of *Dialogues*, tut-tutted as I ran my hand over the poor state of the binding before opening it gently across the support of my lectern. I began to read *the Preface* and realised at once, the full extent of my earlier mistake. That this was the book that might serve as inspiration was at once apparent. I read, *'There was a man of venerable life, blessed by grace, and blessed in name, for he was called "Benedictus" or Benedict. From his younger years, he always had the mind of an old man; for his age was inferior to his virtue*...and so forth, with such captivating and beautiful prose that I could only hope to emulate. My pen scratched on until well into the evening, by which time I had reached the end of Chapter Four, that was, the one where the Saint reformed the monk who would not stay at his prayers.

I rose early the next morning, fired with enthusiasm to continue my research, but first, went to Cuthbert's tomb to report my progress in prayer. I think that this was the day I became obsessed with the task and discovered the patience and received the grace to do it well. All day, I studied Gregory's exchanges with his deacon about the wonderful life of Saint Benedict and made copious notes. Differently from previous days, none of this weighed upon me; indeed, when I reached the end of the thirty-eighth chapter about how a madwoman was cured in the saint's cave and then read the words: *The End, and to God Be the Glory!* my sigh was one of contentment mixed with sadness that Book Two had ended.

I gathered my papers, my tired eyes barely noticing my surroundings as I returned to the small cell at my disposal. After rinsing my face in cold water, I rolled my scribblings tightly and bound them with a ribbon before heading to the refectory to dine. That day I had done without food, being more interested in completing my research, but now my stomach rumbled with hunger.

"Aella! A word if you please." It was a monk, Brother Aelfflaed, with whom I'd had occasional dealings on my first visit to the isle. He smiled at me and placed himself squarely between me and the refectory. "The brothers say that you are working on a volume about the life of our blessed late Bishop Cuthbert."

"That is correct. Except that I have not yet begun the work, as I am collecting the material I need."

The monk, a wiry fellow with sunken cheeks and deep-set eyes, giving him a haunted expression, gave me a cadaverous smile. "That's why I wanted to speak with you, my friend, you see, Cuthbert was much loved and many would willingly contribute. In my case, I was the last person to see Cuthbert alive."

My interest quickened and I begged him to join me over my meal, where he recounted the tale of how he came to be with Cuthbert when he died. "There are other monks who wish to speak of their experiences with our sadly lamented abbot," he informed me and provided a list of names in between mouthfuls of fish soup: "Brother Aethilwald... Plecgils...Tydi and Father Walhstod."

I promised to include his testimony and, when I was ready, to contact each of the monks and the priest he had named.

The next morning, I returned eagerly to the library, where I received an important boost to my confidence. On opening the *Life of St Martin*, the second book on my shortlist, and turning to the *Preface to Desiderius*, I had a surprise. The writer, Sulpicius Severus wrote quite clearly that he had not intended for the book to be circulated because *I am not gifted with much talent, and shrank from the criticisms of the world, lest (as I think will be the case) my somewhat unpolished style should displease my readers.*

Surely then, I need not worry when it came to my efforts that they would be worse than those of Severus? Upon reading his treatise, I soon saw that the chapters were short and that their number, being twenty-seven, would not detain me with note-taking for more than two days. Therefore, a plan came to mind: I would perform this duty conscientiously, then go to the scriptorium to learn about colouring and to collect crystals of gum Arabic and some parchment before returning home for long enough to draw up a structure for my *Vita Sancti Cuthberti*.

NINETEEN

RIDING, NORTHUMBRIA, MAY 687 AD

SUNLIGHT GLINTING OFF A BLADE SPURRED ME TO TAKE A flying leap with a well-judged scissor kick to the side of the villain's head. It sent him sprawling unconscious to the ground, his knife falling harmlessly beside him.

"Aella! Thank God! You saved my life; I couldn't have held the blade off my throat much longer."

"Who is he?" I jerked my thumb at the hulking figure prostrate among the chickweed.

Nerian straightened his tunic and said,

"He ploughs land over yonder, along the Corbridge road a mile or so away. I grind his barley."

"And is that reason enough to want you dead?" I picked up the knife and tucked it in my belt.

My friend laughed mirthlessly,

"He accused me of cheating him."

"And did you?"

"Aella! Of course not!"

I drew my seax since the fellow was stirring.

"I think you'd better explain, Nerian, he's a big brute and he might take persuading that you have the right of it."

The man groaned, rubbed the side of his head and his narrowed eyes directed an evil glare at me before settling on the weapon in my hand.

"I gave him his flour—those two over yonder," he pointed at two pot-bellied sacks on the grass near the path, "and asked for my three sceattas. That's when he drew his knife and went for me."

"Why would he do that if you had ground his corn?"

The dazed man was listening to our exchange but said not a word nor moved.

Nerian spat on the grass, "He said my father ground three sacks with the same amount of grain, which is true. But he wouldn't hear me out, he just lost his temper. After father died, I hoisted the runner stone and dressed it, sharpened the furrowing and improved the feathering." Honestly, it was all so much jargon to me, but I, for one, would hear him out. "Then, I re-set the stone and, as you might suppose, Aella, it grinds finer than in my father's time and I pack more flour into a sack. So, where my father gave him three sacks, I gave him two but asked the same price. He just shouted that I was a cheat and he wouldn't pay three for the price of two. I tried to explain, but he wasn't having any of it!"

I turned my attention to the glowering ceorl,

"Did you hear what the miller said?"

"Ay, but he's trying to swindle folks,"

The glaring fellow pushed himself up onto an elbow and made to rise.

I brandished my seax.

"You'll stay there if you know what's good for you." He sank, supine. "Very wise," I turned to Nerian, "Do you have any other sacks of barley?"

"I do."

"Ready for grinding?"

"They are."

"Good, set your wheel turning and give him a little demonstration."

Nerian hurried to the flume gate and raised it. The mill shuddered as the giant wheel slowly turned.

I reached my left hand over the man on the ground, keeping a firm grasp on my seax whilst he took my hand and I hauled him to his feet.

"Come with me!"

I pushed him in the middle of his back towards the mill.

"Give him one sack of barley, Nerian. Good! Tip the grain where the miller tells you."

"In that hole, right there."

By now, the cogs and shafts were doing their work and the great runner stone was grinding over the fixed bed-stone. The furrows and feathering fulfilled their function and the white powder fell into the hopper and down into the waiting sack. We waited until the flow of flour ceased. The sack under the chute was three-quarters full.

Nerian turned with flashing eyes to the man who had attacked him,

"There, do you believe me now?"

The fellow's expression was sheepish,

"Ay, I do."

"Well, come and check the quality."

"No need for that, I saw it as it came out. Looks like I owe you an apology. And you..." he looked at me and grinned, "...a clout to the head!"

"Hark, old rogue, just thank God I didn't skewer you with your knife whilst you lay senseless at my feet. Be thankful, too, there's no hue and cry out after you, for murder."

"I need to watch my temper, right enough. No hard feelings?"

He fumbled inside his clothing and pulled out a small bag. Shaking out three small silver coins, he handed them to Nerian. I gave him his knife and offered him my hand, which he clasped.

"No hard feelings." I echoed his words and watched him collect his flour and load it onto a small, rickety cart drawn by a sorry-looking donkey. Nerian stopped the flow to the wheel and the whole building seemed to sag to a halt.

"Hark, Aella, will you do me a favour?"

"Another one?" I grinned.

"Ay, well, do you think you could bring Sherlaith here this eve? I've been courting a lass from the village and she's coming here later to sup with my mother and me."

"So, why on earth do you want us to spoil your cosy time together?

He looked mightily embarrassed and said,

"Well, it's like this. I think I love Eawynn and I just thought…"

"Ay?"

"…if she saw you and Sherlaith so happy together…"

"What?"

His face reddened, "…that maybe…well, she might decide she wanted the same."

"That's daft, lad, if you're right for her, you don't need others to set an example."

"I'd like you both to come, anyway," he looked pleadingly, "I know what I'm about. There'll be fresh bread and cakes—"

"All right, just don't get your throat cut in the meantime."

Sherlaith surprised me with her eagerness. I'd never seen her conspiratorial before. She took to the idea of helping Nerian in his love quest as if he were Lugaid.

"But you don't even know him, you goose!"

"Remember I've still got your throwing knife! Anyway, he must be all right, he's a friend of yours."

"Nearly another former friend," I said bitterly.

"What do you mean by that?"

The tale of the knife attack came forth and she listened with increasing amazement.

"So, the people around here aren't all like your family?"

"Honk, honk! I said you were a goose!"

She leapt at me like a wildcat.

After a mock struggle, she quietened.

"Fine example you'd set Nerian's sweetheart!"

Our bickering continued in light-hearted vein until it was time to stroll down the lane to the mill.

Sherlaith and Nerian's maiden made a striking contrast. My wife had lustrous auburn hair worn long as befitting a chieftain's daughter, whilst as a ceorl's offspring, Eawynn's corn blonde locks were cut close, making her oval face impish in appearance. This effect was heightened by her large violet-blue eyes twinkling and this was something the two women shared, their devilry—what Sherlaith called *shenanigans*. Whereas my wife was tall, Eawynn was tiny like a doll and I understood at once why she appealed to my friend. I liked her too, and so did Nerian's mother. If anything, it was he who was tongue-tied and didn't open up until the matter of the afternoon's unpleasantness was raised by Sherlaith.

This was news to the other two women and Nerian was cajoled into telling the tale, ending,

"So, if Aella hadn't chanced by, I wouldn't be here now."

Eawynn had become pale and she twisted her fingers together saying accusingly,

"And you let him go, just like that?"

I gave her a hard stare, "What should I have done? Slaughtered him and been worse than him. He has a family and a poor old donkey!"

At least that made them laugh, but Eawynn flung her arms around Nerian and kissed him passionately.

"I couldn't bear to lose you," she smiled into his shocked face.

"There you are then," Sherlaith twinkled, "it's time you spoke to the maiden's father, Nerian."

"Would that be all right with you, Eawynn?" he asked.

"It would be best, my love."

The rest of the evening passed with us enjoying a splendid meal although I'd be hard put to decide which was more appetising, the fresh bread or the plum cake. Nerian's mother seemed to be beside herself with happiness and I could sympathise. She had not long been a widow and now must be thinking about gaining a daughter to help her and keep her company.

"I like Nerian," Sherlaith said as we followed the moonlit lane home, "But he's too shy. It's clear the lass has lost her head for him."

"Had it been Edwy, they'd already be wed." I mused and by association thought about friendship and Cuthbert. It was precisely at that moment that I knew how I must start my writing, but my best ideas usually come in bed, and Sherlaith didn't let me think about anything but her body that night. Inspired by the experience of the young lovers, she drove us both into a frenzy and I believe, counting backwards, our firstborn was conceived that night.

The next morning, Sherlaith, loath to be separated from me, accompanied me into the nearby woods. She carried her new leather shoulder bag my father had lovingly made for her.

Knowing that she would not want it soiled in any way, I brought along a drawstring cloth bag I scrounged from my mother.

"What do you need that pouch for?" my wife asked.

"I know full well you'll not allow me to put anything in yon bag of yours."

"What would you want to put in it, anyway?"

"Find me an oak tree and I'll tell you!"

"There's one!"

So...there was.

"Let's have a contest, see who can collect the most oak apples"—by which I meant oak galls, those hard, round balls produced by a wasp in the place of acorns.

"Here's one!" she pounced, "one to me nought to you!"

After an hour we had collected sufficient for my purposes, which I refused to divulge, just to torment her. Sherlaith wasn't one to contain her curiosity.

"What do you want them for?"

"All in good time, Ser-la!"

"Oofah!"

"Look there's a tumbledown shed over there, let's see who can pull out more rusty nails."

She looked sulky but intrigued. "You collect them yourself! I'm not ruining my hands."

It was an easy task to ease the nails, exposed by fallen-away planks, out of the rotting wood. She couldn't resist and passed me a couple she'd worked loose.

"Right, I think we can go back," I said.

"Aren't you going to tell me?"

"I am not, but I promise you can watch what I'm about."

We went back to my father's workshop and I found a hammer and proceeded to shock her by smashing the tough oak galls into tiny pieces.

"Did we go to all that trouble just so that you could destroy them?"

"Exactly!"

My father looked up from slicing leather and grinned. He knew what I was doing, but joined in the teasing.

"Oh, I've *no* idea," he said with a smirk when she asked him.

"Oh, you can tell me, *faither*" she wheedled, increasing her brogue.

But he said he couldn't and she stamped her foot.

"Will you cover the base of this old pan with vinegar, my love?"

She snatched at the handle and stormed off to ask my mother for the liquid.

"I think you'd better tell her when she comes back," Oswin suggested sensibly.

But there was no need, she reappeared with a broad grin, "You're making ink!"

"Women! You simply have to know everything. You can help. Put the rusty nails in the vinegar."

I selected another pan, covered the oak galls with water and placed it over the fire to simmer for half an hour.

"This is the last thing." I waved a small vial of amber-coloured crystals at her, "Pass me that small pan, please," and into it, I shook some crystals and added water, "gum arabic," I explained, it's a glue and acts as a binder, so the ink won't fade."

After three days, the solutions were ready and I was able to strain the bits out of the gall solution before mixing the three potions into ink. I cut across a quill to make a nib and cutting off a strip of parchment wrote, *I love you, Sherlaith.*

Giving it to her, she stared uncomprehendingly and when I read it for her, she squealed with delight and stuffed the scrap of parchment into her treasured shoulder bag. Now, I was ready to begin the first page of my book and didn't need to be on Lindisfarena to do it.

TWENTY

I BEGAN MY ACCOUNT OF CUTHBERT'S LIFE WITH AN earnest eulogy and followed it with my theory that he was born in Ériu, the son of a noble father. Later, as he told me, loving foster parents raised him in Northumbria. I soon wrote this in my best handwriting and it filled but a few pages. When I had finished, I explained to Sherlaith my need to be alone in the hope that I could recall my friend's exact words through meditation.

The mellow late-spring sunlight caressing the sandstone of Edwy's Cross and the reeling song of a skulking warbler transported me once more to the cove we shared on Lindisfarena. I closed my eyes and conjured the vision of Cuthbert drinking in the lapping waves with his gaze and toying with a spindly sea thrift. In my mind, I heard him say,

"My earliest memory, you ask, Aella? There was one remarkable occurrence as I recall. I was eight years old and in the habit of seeking playmates of my age as youngsters are wont to do. Among my peers, it is fair to say, I was the most agile and high-spirited. I honestly believe I surpassed them all. Oh, look, Aella is that not a seal bobbing in the sea, yonder?"

The wonders of the world around him forever distracted Cuthbert and as always, he returned gently to the point of our discussion.

"Ah yes, this particular day many youths gathered on a field of level ground, perfect for a playground and we began to do cartwheels, handstands and all manner of other tricks. Nothing remarkable in all that, you will say, my friend..."

Never one to rush into an affirmation, I pondered for a moment and he smiled sweetly. At last, I said,

"I would say not."

"One of the youths had brought along his little brother, a child with but three winters to his name. As usual, I had surpassed the others in enterprising leaps and prodigious handstands when all of a sudden in a deep and adult voice, the child remonstrated with me. Aella, believe me, to hear a little one speaking with a man's voice is a shocking thing..." he fell into one of those faraway reveries that I had grown familiar with, where his eyes stared unseeingly into the distance and a trance-like stillness enveloped him.

Whenever this happened, I dared not disturb him, for it would have been an intrusion and I feel sure that he appreciated my company and also my sensibility. This time, neither gesture nor so much as a cough on my part regained his attention but suddenly he continued.

"The child used words a three-year-old could not possibly have learnt," a tone of awe entered his voice that made the hairs on my arms prickle. "Cuthbert," the child admonished, *'be steadfast and leave this foolish play...'*" my friend heaved a sigh and turned his awestruck gaze upon me, "well, I'm ashamed to say that I ignored him and he began to weep and would not cease until I stopped my cavorting. When I went over to this mere babe, he looked at me and, inconsolable, tears flooded down his face. Then, again with the same disturbing voice he addressed me thus, '*Cuthbert, bishop and priest, cease this vainglory! Your lack of humility shames you in the eyes of the Lord.*' Can you imagine, Aella, these words from the mouth of a babe? Are we not told, by the Apostle, Matthew, that the Lord said, '*Out of the mouth of babes and nursing infants you have perfected praise*'? I thought of this in later years, Aella, but that child pre-announced my vocation and foresaw that I would indeed, become a priest and a bishop."

Again, he was lost to me as he drifted into some faraway world of his own imaginings. Just as I, hearing the squealing of a cartwheel, returned to my world by the stone cross to exchange a carter's cheery greeting. Such had been my concentration that when I stood, my head spun and I feared I'd forget all that I had recalled. To prevent this from happening, I hurried home and wrote the tale of the three-year-old as I'd heard it from Cuthbert's mouth.

Sherlaith sought me out later and having just finished the account, I gave her all my attention. I had decided what to do next, but it required a little effort and if she so chose, my wife could be of help.

"Ser-la, would you care to lend me a hand?"

She looked quizzical and smiled, which I took to mean assent.

"Today, there's pleasant sunshine. Take this drawstring bag and see if you can collect more than a score of ladybirds."

She couldn't resist prying, of course.

"What do you want them for?"

"My work. You're more inquisitive than the cat. And it's forever delving where it shouldn't! Heed me, I'm taking the horse to the coast and won't be back till late afternoon."

"Why?"

I laughed, ignored the question and mounted the steady old nag we'd bought on the other coast.

I smiled down at her, "To buy a bag of whelks."

I nudged my mount away just as she asked, "What for?"

"You'll see!"

When I got back, she greeted me with the linen bag I'd given her.

"A score-and-ten," she held it out and snatched it away as I reached to take it.

"Nay! Not until you tell me why you want them."

I grinned at her, "It's the least you deserve, my love, for your fine effort. They are to provide me with colour for my book. The ladybirds can surrender their red—it's a tint known as carmine—I learnt the trick from the Lindisfarena monks.

She put the bag behind her back, "You're going to kill the poor darlings, aren't you?"

"Ser-la, you're talking to a man who has killed other men in battle. Do you think I'll hold back from crushing a few insects, however pretty they might be? Besides, my book is for the glory of an extraordinarily holy man. Now, give it here!"

Reluctantly, she passed the bag and to spare her feelings, I didn't squash the bugs there and then. Instead, to involve her, I explained why I had gone to the coast. I held up a bag of whelks and, taking one out, put it on the bench and hit the shell with a hammer. Carefully removing the pieces of the outer casing, I exposed the mollusc and just as the scribe on the isle had said, I located a gland where a clear, slightly yellow mucus, interacting with the air, began to change colour before our eyes. We watched it, fascinated as first, it became green, then blue, followed by blue-violet and, finally, red-purple.

"Look, Ser-la, the Romans used this secretion to dye cloth. I'm going to use it to paint. I have most of my colours and the gum arabic to bind them. There's madder in the ground behind the house for a dark red, your ladybirds for bright red, there's still some orpiment from Hexham for yellow and I can mix it with woad to obtain green. The woad will give me blue..." my enthusiasm caused me to launch into this long list. My wife fixed me with a stare of twinkling devilment.

"And yet, husband, you have forgotten a vital colour for your art."

I frowned, surely, I had named all the important ones?

"You're thinking of gold, maybe?"

"Nay."

Her teasing was working. I cared too much for the book and feared to fall into error. I thought of all the colours in the world.

"Pink?"

She was about to shake her head when, thanks to pink, it came to me.

"*White!* That's it! I can't make pink without white. But I was coming to that."

Sherlaith was grinning broadly.

"What? Did you think I'd forgotten it?"

"Well, you didn't mention white."

I pinched her arm gently, "Only because you interrupted me in full flow! I'll need vinegar to make white."

"You'll use up all your poor mother's vinegar! There'll be none left for cooking."

"My painting's more important. If *you* ask her, she won't say no."

I needed the vinegar to soak a piece of lead so that it would corrode. That's what the monk had told me. To complete the operation, I'd have to rely on my horse.

"Put fresh horse dung into the lead and vinegar and a small miracle happens," the brother had said, "it converts the white corrosion into beautiful white flakes, ready to be made into a paint."

When I'd produced all my pigments, I chose a piece of parchment and trimmed it to size for my book. The sketch was conceived as follows: in the background, a simple house with a dark red-tiled roof, resting on four columns, which would be white; to the right, Cuthbert kneeling in prayer and I would paint his cloak dark blue and his tunic, red. Dominating the scene, his horse reaching up to the roof and pulling down a linen bag. The whole painting, I would enclose in a golden frame. This would illustrate the second tale Cuthbert had told me about his youth and I remembered it in every detail because it had made a great impression on me.

My tongue between my teeth, my brush strokes carefully delineating the scene, I had reached the swirling green grass in the foreground when Sherlaith peered over my shoulder.

"You *are* good, aren't you! What does the picture show, a man and his horse?"

I set my brush down, took a deep breath and began,

"The man is Cuthbert when he was young and you see him praying. He was travelling on a horse from the south and had just crossed the River Wear when a terrible rainstorm caught them. He told me they came to some dwellings used only in spring and summer and given that it was winter, they were deserted. Wearied by the journey and hungry, seeking shelter, Cuthbert led his horse into one of them. Unsaddling the beast, and fastening it to a wall, he decided to wait for the storm to pass. Devout as ever, he knelt, as you see here and prayed to the Lord and whilst he was doing so, saw his steed raise its head to the roof—as I've painted—and greedily seize part of the thatch, drawing it towards him. Cuthbert believed the animal was trying to eat the thatch, but from the straw fell out a linen cloth containing warm bread and meat wrapped in more linen…"

Sherlaith's eyes widened, "That was a miracle!"

"Indeed, and that's the whole point of the book, to the glory of God and Cuthbert."

My wife looked suitably impressed, so I added,

"Cuthbert told me that the food was sent by God through an angel who helped him whenever he was in serious difficulties. So, before leaving, he thanked God, blessed the food, shared some bread with his horse and, satisfied and strengthened, he continued on his journey."

"Will you write this tale?"

"Ay, in Latin and remember, Ser-la, it's for King Aldfrith to read when I'm done. But it will take a while because I have to divide the volume into four books, each referred to different periods of Cuthbert's life. This first book is about his youth." I told her the tale of the three-year-old and my ideas for the next pages after this account of the horse.

"When I've finished these tales of his youth, I'll have to go back to Lindisfarena to report my progress and show my work to Abbot Eadberht. Also, I'll need to seek out those who knew him in his later life."

"It's going to be a long task."

"Many years, I'd say."

She looked at me with a strange pinched expression,

"Well, you can't leave for Lindisfarena just yet."

"Why not?"

"I have an idea that Nerian will be organising a feast very soon!" she said before leaving me to work in peace.

This was correct, as an hour later, Nerian came bounding into my workshop like a hound off a leash.

"Aella! What do you think? I'm to be wed! You and your family are all invited to the celebrations."

"Congratulations! When?"

"A month to this very day. What do you think of Eawynn?"

He looked anxiously into my face as if what I thought mattered.

"There's no bonnier lass in the village. You chose well. How did her father react?"

"Oh, he's pleased. The mill provides a good living and he knows his girl will not go without. Do you know what he said? He wanted his elder daughter Merwen, you know, the one who married the smith, to wed our Edwy, but well, you know…" he ended sorrowfully. Anyway, I'd better get on, others to invite. I wanted to ask you first—"

"Ask him what?"

We spun around. Sherlaith had re-entered the workshop.

"If you'd come to our wedding feast."

"Oh, Nerian, I'm so happy for you both!" she beamed, "of course we'll come," she took his hand, and looking embarrassed for speaking out of turn, shot me a sideways glance, "won't we, Aella?"

"We will, and I'm sure my parents will be delighted to come, too. Let's go and tell them."

On reflection, there seemed little point in hurrying to Lindisfarena just to come back straight away, besides my time with Sherlaith was precious. Not that I was wasting any time neglecting the king's book. During the month, I wrote the tale of Cuthbert's vision of the soul of Aidan, bishop of Lindisfarena, being borne to heaven by an angel at the precise moment of the prelate's death. I penned several other miracles of his youth and spent the three days before the wedding painting Cuthbert washing the feet of an angel disguised as a pilgrim. In reality, this was out of place because I intended it for Book II, but I wanted a break from writing. I think my head was less on Latin and more on Nerian's feast.

TWENTY-ONE

THERE'S A SAYING OFTEN REPEATED IN THESE PARTS: *things come in threes.* It was certainly the case on Nerian and Eawynn's hand-binding day. Apart from the official love-match, two other pleasant surprises awaited me that evening. Nerian's mother, an exemplary cook, devoted herself as never before to ensuring everything was perfect for her son and his bride. The table groaned under bowls of beans and barley flavoured with mint and thyme, followed by mixed platters of roasted swine, wild fowls, hare and eels. All this we washed down with a choice of ale, cider or mead. The room resounded to laughter, voices raised in merriment and repeated toasts to the couple.

Then came the first of the surprises, the admirable cook silenced everybody by approaching the table with her showpiece on a tray. She had roasted a large fowl and contrived to leave in place its long neck, and head complete with its sword-like bill—a heron.

Like most people feasting that evening, I had never eaten heron and was curious. That particular bird is a silent killer, waiting motionless as a statue standing in the water before, in a flash, striking to grab its prey in that long, dagger-like beak. It feeds on small fish and frogs, so I should have imagined its meat would be *gamey*. Nerian carved the breast, heeding his mother's advice not to serve other parts of the fowl.

"I'd noticed this beast standing in the river just upstream of the mill. It's been here on and off for some weeks. So yesterday I took my bow and got close without scaring it and my aim was true. The rest is down to mother," Nerian announced.

Sherlaith and I were discussing our opinion of heron meat when she leant close and whispered in my ear.

"I missed my bleed last month."

Amid the din around me, I wasn't sure I'd heard correctly and asked her to repeat her words. I was not mistaken. Excited, I put my mouth to her ear and whispered, "How sure are you?"

"I never normally miss, Aella; anyway, I've been feeling sick in the morning—it's a sure sign."

I was thrilled and secretly hoped for a son. If my wish was granted, I already had a name in mind. I stared at Nerian, his face alight with joy and looking for all the world as I remembered Edwy in his carefree moments.

Sherlaith nudged me and did her usual trick of reading my thoughts.

"Of course, it might be a girl."

"And if it is, I shall adore her even more than her mother. Ow!"

My jest had earned me a sharp and well-deserved elbow in the ribs. But nothing could stop me thinking that I was as close to heaven as I would ever come on this earth.

Wishing to show Sherlaith the boundlessness of my joy at her news with a gift, I rose with the dawn, despite our late-night festivities, saddled my horse and rode off to Hexham. Even as I approached the town, I had no idea what I would buy for her. Behind the abbey, in the area occupied by the stonemasons, I remembered that other craftsmen toiled. I directed my horse there, acting on a vague notion that I might find something suitable. Dismounting and tying my patient beast to a rail, I picked my way through the filth of the street until I came to a line of workshops. The first was a basket-weaver's, which I ignored since we had enough baskets of all sizes and for different uses. Anyway, I was looking for something with charm and more personal. The weaver's delayed me for a moment and I was tempted by a colourful shawl—but my joy at the arrival of a child required something less mundane.

I found what I was looking for in a carver's workshop. He had a display of pendant crosses, carved from different materials: bone, antler, ivory and jet. There were also silver and gold ones but my purse wouldn't allow such luxury. I studied the jewels made from less precious substances. They shared the same basic design, with the arms of equal length and narrower at the centre. The carver, sitting behind a bench, knife in one hand and a piece of antler in the other, looked up and smiled.

"Them's what we call *'footed crosses'*, see them's broad at the outer edges." He was saying what I could see plainly for myself. He had carved them with a loop on the upper arm for threading a string or chain. "The black ones are jet from Whitby, down the coast. Jet's hard to come by and worth good coin." He laid down what he was working with and wandered over. "see, that's just plain bone, them's ivory and them there's a copper alloy."

I picked up the black cross, fascinated by its lustrous radiance.

"Ay, that's the Whitby jet. It's a protection against the evil eye; it draws the wickedness into itself, to keep the wearer safe. Look closely and you'll see the work that's gone into it."

It was true, being black, the sculpting wasn't immediately apparent but on inspection, there was the figure of Christ holding a book and it had the same-shaped cross on its cover. That decided me. Here was all the protection my darling Sherlaith might need and it was a beautiful gift.

Not given to arguing over price, I handed over the silver pieces the fellow asked for without quibbling, also because I admired his craftsmanship. He pointed out that my wife would need something to thread through it else how would she wear it? I'd completely forgotten. But I refused various cheap laces that only detracted from the beauty of the cross and opted for a finely-wrought silver chain with an overlap clasp.

I have always found the pleasure of giving more thrilling than receiving, so anticipation made the ride home cheerful. Sherlaith, who had been asleep when I left home, was at the gate, on the lookout for my return.

"Where have you been?"

In truth, her curiosity was as bad as the cat's! I laughed heartily, then said,

"If you really must know, I've been to Hexham to buy a gift for you: I'm so pleased with your news."

She bounced on the balls of her feet, "A gift!"

At times she was like a little girl and I loved her for it.

From that day onwards, she was never seen without her footed cross. There was a second motive for why I had gone out of my way to purchase the pendant; I wanted her to forgive me for going away again. There was no reason why I couldn't continue the *Life of St Cuthbert* from home but I was well aware of King Aldfrith's interest and the pressure he would be applying to the elderly abbot of Lindisfarena. I thought that if I could show Eadberht my work, he would be able to reassure the king about its progress. He would understand, if he didn't already, how much time the task would need.

The bitter-sweet leave-taking over, I set off for the holy isle —the destination of pilgrims intent on visiting the shrine of Saint Cuthbert but also the relic of St Oswald's head, recently housed there. Thus, I found myself, for the first time, amid a crowd of noisy travellers waiting for the tide to ebb sufficiently for our passage.

I had to wait for an audience with the abbot, but when the elderly monk admitted me to his quarters, he was eager to see my efforts. I sat quietly awaiting his judgement and it proved worthwhile because he bestowed the most wonderful smile upon me and complimented me on the correctness of my Latin and my skill as an illuminator.

"Father Abbot, I loved Cuthbert as a brother, and am putting my whole heart into this work."

"And it shows, my son. It will please me to tell King Aldfrith what a splendid manuscript you are producing for him."

"There is one thing..."

He cocked his head, like a hound capturing a distant sound.

"...I should like to work from home as I have done thus far, since my wife is with child."

He beamed, "The Lord be praised! It is His blessing in return for your devotion. You may work wherever suits you best, my son. Ask if there is anything you need."

So concluded a most satisfactory audience. But I could not yet hurry home to my family because I was aware of the gaps in my knowledge about Cuthbert. Lindisfarena a small community and despite the large number of pilgrims, my meeting with the abbot was soon the talk of the refectory. Happily, some monks wished to share their memories of

Cuthbert with me. I do not suppose there was a single brother on the isle who did not know what I was doing. So, that very afternoon, a monk called Baldhelm approached me.

"Brother Aella," he began and I did not correct him about my status since I carried out the work of a monastic scribe, "I wish to talk to you about the sainted Cuthbert." And so, he recounted his time as a servant of a rich man named Sibba and of a miracle that Cuthbert performed at his house. I took the monk to the scriptorium and wrote down detailed notes, for this tale would fill a gap in my future book IV. I had been worrying about the blank period that coincided with my time at Lismore Abbey in Ériu. This was a big help and I blessed Brother Baldhelm for it, begging him to circulate word of my need for similar accounts of the last years of my friend's life. For this reason, I resolved to await what the next day might bring.

Four different testimonies were forthcoming and it took me all day to hear the tales and check the details whilst writing my notes. Confident that the content of Book IV would be as thorough as the others, I decided to depart for home on the morrow. One factor that reassured me about the last book was that I was in an ongoing situation. I had discovered that miracles were occurring regularly at Cuthbert's shrine. Each new wonder would be a candidate for inclusion and as I estimated years rather than months to the conclusion of my opus, further prodigies might well be forthcoming.

TWENTY-TWO

MY HOMECOMING, AS SWEET AS I IMAGINED, PRESENTED me with a dilemma. I envied the Lindisfarena copyists whose labour simply involved reproducing and illustrating gospels already inscribed. I wondered if Gregory the Great and Sulpicius Severus, who like me had written *ex novo*, had wrestled with the same tormenting doubts I was experiencing. Had I completed Book I? Were there serious omissions or could I improve the contents? In this state of mind, there were two solutions I could fall back on: meditation or stalling.

Since I believe that Time is a great counsellor, I opted for the latter. To do this, without wasting time, I retrieved my illustration prepared in anticipation of Book II, gnashed my teeth and tore it to pieces. Only my best would do for the king. I still wanted to illustrate that particular scene, but to do it more effectively, maybe I needed to write the tale first. In Book II, Cuthbert had become a monk and I wished to relate all the episodes he had recounted about the cloistered life. Where better to begin than with his experience while still a neophyte at the monastery of Ripon? This was the story behind the illustration I'd just shredded.

I sharpened a new quill, dipped it in ink and scratched away. Re-reading my effort, I was tempted to consign it to the same fate as the doomed image. But just as I was about to tear the pages across, a thought stilled my hands. Was my dissatisfaction due to something that could not be captured in writing, especially not in the formal language of Latin? As I had set down the tale, I remembered with fondness Cuthbert's emotions during the telling—and that was something cold narration could never capture. Besides, if I began to shred every one of my efforts, the king, who was older than me, might never receive the book in his lifetime! I read the account again aloud, translating as I went into my everyday tongue:

"Cuthbert's job at Ripon was to greet guests at the monastery. As usual, he washed and rubbed the feet of one weary traveller and his next thought was to feed him. Searching the kitchen of the guesthouse and its pantry, he discovered there was no bread..." So far, so good, I thought and read on, "...To rectify the situation, the young monk hurried to the monastery, but because the bread there was still baking, sadly he had to return empty-handed; when Cuthbert returned, the visitor—an angel in disguise—had vanished leaving three warm loaves." I sighed, satisfied that I'd covered everything Cuthbert had told me, but sorrowful that I hadn't been able to render the feeling of awe that the young Cuthbert had experienced at the sight of the gift. My sadness did not last because Sherlaith, who unknown to me had been listening as I translated.

"That's astonishing," she said, and there was awe in her voice, "a miracle. God sent an angel to Cuthbert."

Her tone and wide-eyed wonder soothed all my worries; for it meant I had achieved what I'd set out to do, my wife having given me the most unbiased of judgements. This incident perked me up and I laid aside the newly written first pages of Book II, stood to gather my colours and redrafted the illustration. Suitably inspired, the sketch pleased me far more than my first attempt and I began to apply colour. I worked all day on it and most of the next morning until I put the last touches to the golden outline of the frame. I sat back and admired my effort.

This time, I had created a tall building in the background to represent the monastery and given it a green-tiled roof. To create the illusion of space, two thin columns ran in parallel and next to the frame. They supported a triple arch which, in the foreground, delineated the room where Cuthbert tended the angel. I depicted the heavenly creature sitting on the edge of a bed and wearing a dark blue tunic, around his head shone a halo, lest there be any doubt to his nature; the spiritual visitor is bent forward slightly over the kneeling monk, his hands open and outspread, whilst quite clearly from his back sprouted two angelic wings. One of his feet was in an earthenware bowl whereas Cuthbert was drying the other and looking up into the guest's face. The young monk was wearing a brown habit with the hood pulled up but not covering his earnest face.

I leant back in my chair and considered myself satisfied with my effort. Packing my colours away, I then stood and wandered over to peer at what my father was doing. For once, Oswin was not slicing or stitching leather, but planing the edges of a rectangle of beech.

"What are you doing, father?"

"Saving you time, my lad."

"What do you mean?"

He turned over the piece of wood and used the plane to slope the edges.

"I'm making the cover for your book. I saw the size of your pages and thought I'd help."

"Well, it's very good of you but the book won't be ready for at least two years. And I haven't given any thought to cover design."

"If it's for the king, you'll need a well-worked binding."

"Ay, that I will."

"You'll have plenty of time to sort that out, but if you want me to work from a design, I can do that."

I was flooded by a warm feeling of affection for my father. I knew that he could work leather even better than I, perhaps what he lacked was a spark of creativity. If I drew up a template for him, he could do the work and save me weeks of meticulous incising.

"When I've thought it through, I'll give you the pattern, father, and you can do the king's cover." I was rewarded with the most loving smile he'd ever bestowed on me. All in all, life could not treat me better—and, unless I was mistaken, from the kitchen came the unmistakable aroma of eel stewing. Whether it would be eel pie or stew mattered not as I loved either one. Nerian had brought the eels yesterday as his traps had proved so effective; my friend had much to thank the river for.

Now I had finished the first tale and its illustration to Book II, I thought I might stroll over to the mill for a chat with the newly-wed miller. On the way, I'd stop at Edwy's Cross to sit and think about the cover design and the next tale to be written.

The first swallows of the year were scything through the air and making their amazing swoops to avoid the stone cross. I watched them entranced and inspiration came. It had nothing to do with birds and owed everything to relaxation and happiness. My thoughts had strayed to my wife and her pleasure at receiving the pendant cross. By association, I thought of its creator, the craftsman in Hexham, and had a flash of inventiveness. What if my father were to stitch around inserts made of other material? In my mind's eye, I saw a petal-shaped rhomboid at the centre delineated by a lacework of small pearls and within this frame a carved ivory miniature portraying Cuthbert at prayer. The corners could contain other miniatures, but what about the cost? Would I have the courage to go to Babbanburgh to ask the king for money?

I leapt to my feet, abandoning the plan of calling on Nerian, and ran back to our workshop. Seizing a piece of parchment, I took a stick of charcoal and sketched out the semblance of my idea. My father was staring at me, his curiosity aroused by my frenetic activity.

"What're you up to, lad?"

I picked up the parchment and carried it over to him.

"I think this can be done. These are small pearls and they can be set into the leather and this could be ivory and these, either ivory or jet."

"Not jet, ivory."

"So, if I can get this design, in more detail, of course, to a carver I know in Hexham, would you be able to inlay the miniatures?"

My father looked at me and his lip curled,

"What about some rubies while you're at it?"

He was being sarcastic, but what if the king wanted jewels? In any case, he'd made his point.

"I'll have to see what the king thinks of the idea. I'll paint an impression of what the finished work will look like. The important thing is that it can be done."

"You'll have to get your ivory carver to make the discs with some thin tongues that I can slot into the leather, to help hold his work in place."

"That should be no problem. First, I'll take the idea to King Aldfrith and see what he thinks."

Three days later, I stood in the king's hall, clutching my rolled parchment, waiting for him to finish a hearing to settle a land dispute. The wrangling went on for some time until the king's patience was exhausted. A look of barely controlled rage replaced his usual benign temper and he exerted his authority with decisiveness.

As the plaintiffs bowed out of the hall, I hoped the king would be in cordial enough mood to discuss my work.

As it happened, he transferred his furious glower to me and momentarily I felt as I had before the onrushing Picts. But just as the sun returns from behind a cloud, so his face brightened.

"Ah, Master Aella. What news of your *Cuthbert*? Abbot Eadberht tells me you are making excellent progress."

He smiled and his eyes strayed to the parchment rolled tightly in my hand.

"The volume will be in four books, Sire, and I have completed Book One. I come today with an idea for the cover because that, too, will take time and much precise work. May I?" I brandished the rolled parchment.

"Step this way!" The king led me to a table where I unrolled the design.

"It is only a flat rendition, Lord, the pearls and ivory will have their natural lustre that my poor hand cannot imitate, but I think it gives the idea."

"It is an ingenious ploy, Master Aella, to embellish the leather and make it more precious. Are these then carvings of scenes from the life of the saint?"

"They are, Sire."

"And you have come here today for my approval. Ay, well, indeed you have it. Remarkable!"

Despite the splendid acceptance, I must have looked

discomfited and the sharp-eyed king noticed.

"Was there anything else, Master Aella?"

"Forgive me, Sire, but there is the cost of the materials and the carver to consider."

The distinguished-looking monarch laughed and said, "As we speak, a...let's call it...a whim...takes my fancy. What say you, Master, if we place a ruby here, here, here and here?"

I smiled at my father's sardonic jest of several days before.

"Sire, the leather can be disposed to receive the gems and the final sealing will be done by my hand in your presence if you so desire.

"I do!" The ruler turned and waved a hand at one of his counsellors and gave instructions to fetch a purse of coins.

Until I was out of the hall, out of the town itself, I had no idea of how generous the king had been. It is unwise to flourish money bags within the sight of people, so finding an isolated spot, I drew open the purse and discovered a small fortune in gold and silver coins. True, the king had said that the coin would cover the craftsman's wage but was also payment for my production of the volume. Even so, it was a gift of great generosity. I hid the money bag safely out of sight and resumed my journey to Riding.

I decided to stop off at home before continuing to Hexham the next day. There was no particular rush and I had no doubt whatsoever that the carver would accept the royal commission. Whistling merrily and thinking about the *Vita Sancti Cuthberti* as I marched, I hit upon the idea of a white lie. What if I gave father a gold coin and told him that the king required him to make the cover? There was no harm in such friendly deceit and it would make Oswin proud and happy. He need not know about the rest of the small fortune—that was my business. And how I was going to enjoy teasing my father about those rubies!

TWENTY-THREE

HEXHAM, NORTHUMBRIA, JULY 687 AD

THE ABBEY CHIMES ASSAULTED MY EARDRUMS. THERE IS something intolerable, unignorable, about church bells at close quarters. They began their clamour just when I approached the building meaning to pass by its right-hand side. As if commanded by them, I mounted the steps and entered the place of worship. The solid walls provided refuge for my still ringing ears. Outside the insistent rhythmic clangour continued and inside another sense was assailed. The thin curling grey waves of incense reminded me of impermanence, the transience of the soul or purification, but the cloying sweetness of spice made my head spin. Rather like flotsam, I was swept along by a greater force to complete my sensual buffeting before a painting on the north wall of the abbey. The sun was painted black and the moon, crimson like blood, while the stars were falling to earth.

Standing back from the image, my stricken senses reeling, I recognised what was happening to me. The Church was assailing my agitated bodily organs to impose its values. In the absence of bells, they might choose to belabour my ears with the intonation of prayers or the reverberations of chanted psalms. Pummelling my eyes now, was a scene I recognised from my studies at Lismore: from the Revelations of St John— the idea, I supposed, being to make me examine my conscience with severity.

I swallowed hard and began to reason. It was difficult to believe that much time before I had been a pagan. My conversion had been casual and unconvincing, but after years of study and, above all the fortune of associating with a true man of God, I had become a devout Christian. Or had I? Was it more that I had grown profoundly in love with His Creation as Cuthbert had taught me, capable of seeing Heaven in a wild flower?

Oblivious to my surroundings, desperate only for unconfined space, but out of decorum I restrained myself from hurtling outdoors. Once in front of the edifice, instead of pursuing my original intention to seek out the craftsman, I headed for the river, gratefully leaving the church bells behind along with the clamour and bustle of the town, needing silence and fresh air.

Sitting on the grassy bank, I restored my calm by watching the swallows skim less than an inch above the surface of the water, with its starburst flashes of sunlight, and hearing from on high the mew of a gull and the distant, now innocuous, even restful, peal of the bells.

Everything has a purpose, a meaning, I thought, trying to understand what had happened to me. One moment, I was striding towards a craftsman's workshop, the next, I found myself unwittingly directed into the abbey, to come under sensory attack—like a warrior in a shield-wall under a hail of missiles but without a shield! I smiled grimly at my fanciful comparison. What was the meaning of all this?

Running through my reasons for being in Hexham, the

reason for it came to me. The fear of falling below the standard deserving of a king, or worthy of a saint, had made me so inexplicably receptive to the sensations propounded by the Church. The cover of the *Vita* would, in miniature, have to replicate a similar vivid evocation upon the senses of the aspiring reader. The rolled parchment I had clutched throughout my experience seemed woefully inadequate and yet it had received the king's approval. I rose slowly and strolled thoughtfully back towards the workshops behind the abbey.

The clang of hammers, barking dogs, the foul odour of excrement, none of these disturbed me although, once home in Riding, I would not miss them. The bustle of activity increased, as was normal, in proximity to the abbey but nothing distracted me from my purpose. The realisation that my earlier fear was partially induced by the necessity to cede control was dominating my thoughts. Regarding the *Vita*, it was I who would write the text; mine the hand to paint the images; my father to shape the leather binding—which was almost the same as it being me, but now I had committed myself to another extraneous hand. As I approached his workshop, I reasoned that I had seen, handled and been impressed by his craftsmanship. The question that troubled me was the extent that I, as one artisan would be able to prevail upon another. This thought resulted in my breezing into his work place and tossing one of the king's gold coins on the bench in front of him.

It might not have been the happiest of ploys. Like a cat stroked against the lie of its fur, he spat,

"What's the meaning of this?"

Trying to ignore the hostility in his voice, I said,

"It's for you, my friend," and in an attempt to soothe him,

"I was delighted by the workmanship in the footed cross you sold me last week, remember?"

"Ay, the jet one."

"That's it. I at once thought of you for the king's work. The coin's meant as a sum in advance."

He stared hard at me, still ignoring the coin that lay untouched where I'd placed it.

"The king? What do you want of me? I'm a busy man."

"But not too occupied for King Aldfrith's needs, I'll warrant."

He glared at me, "You wander in here like you own the place, stick gold under my nose and issue your orders—"

I held both hands up in a sign of submission and tried to look contrite.

"You are right, my friend. I am so taken with the task charged me that I forgot myself. I beg your pardon and wish to be clear that I have come to seek your unequalled skills to be the crowning glory of my commission for the king."

His interest was piqued and I had elicited half a smile with my flattery.

"And what work would that be?"

"I, too, am a craftsman, but my material is leather..." I went on to describe what I was doing and how the finished volume would be bound. Next, I explained what I foresaw as his contribution.

Circumspectly, I sought his permission, accorded, to spread the parchment on his bench. The atmosphere of tension had evaporated like early morning dew.

He studied my design for a while, frowned, muttered to himself, then smiled into my face,

"There's no problem making the plaques as you request. Only I think flanges rather than tongues would be better for fixing, you see that'd give more permanence, less chance of snapping." His finger stabbed the painting, "And I'm not keen on that!"

He pointed to what I considered the highlight of the cover, the central petal.

"What's wrong with it? The shape?"

"No, the shape's fine. It's the content. You can't have that monk there; it has to be Our Lord in Splendour. Come with me and I'll show you."

He took me over to an ivory sculpture, probably part of a box to house a relic or similar, the craftsmanship was exquisite and I felt further reassured by my choice of the artist. The image showed Christ on a throne, his right hand raised in benediction, his left supporting a book with a cross on the cover on His thigh. Under and bearing the ceremonial seat, on either side, were two angels looking outwards, whilst above two others in flight steadied it. I was looking at a wonderful piece of work without discussion, but I said,

"It's magnificent, Master, but my book is about the monk, not Christ."

"What do monks signify unless service to Christ?"

His tone was cutting, come here!"

Obediently, I returned to my design, where his finger was already pointing.

"And these are no good." He tapped the four shapes in the corners, "No, my friend, what you need here are roundels. Your praying monk can go in the bottom right corner—for that's the last place the eye will rest before the book is opened. The beholder will see Christ in Majesty first, then move to the top-left roundel, where it will encounter my snakes intertwining and biting their own bodies: a clear sign that this volume of yours is made for a king since the serpents demand respect and confer authority, a suitable symbol for a ruler."

As I had feared, my craftsman had taken control of the

work, but there was sense and beauty in what he proposed. He took me across the workshop to show me designs for the other two roundels and explained their significance. For one, he suggested a very intricate design with a monogram but with such a proliferation of infilled scrollwork as almost to baffle the normal function of reading.

"Can you not make out the letters?" he seemed offended.

"Well, there's a C and isn't that an H and this an I?"

He laughed, "It's Greek, and look here— R-H-O. Ah, I see you have no Greek, my friend Chi-Rho: the first two letters in that language word for Christ. You'll find it in the abbey, for sure."

"I know Latin," I grumbled to soothe my hurt pride.

In his proposal for the remaining roundel, I saw rather an undecipherable thicket of interlaced animals, yet fluid and graceful. I made out their ring and dot eyes, birds' hooked beaks and the four-toed feet of a dog-like creature.

"These will represent God's creatures and His Creation."

Given that it was one of Cuthbert's most beloved themes, there was no point in resisting. If my father and I could insert this fellow's work into our leatherwork, it would indeed be fit for the king.

Established that my template was full-size, we clasped hands on our contract. He promised to have the five miniatures ready in exactly one year. In return, I pledged a second gold coin of the same value upon receipt of the work.

However, I could not leave without satisfying my curiosity.

"Where do you procure your ivory, Master?"

He reached below the bench and using both hands, picked up and deposited six tusks on it.

"Walrus tusks," I buy them from a trader who works the far northern seas. "He doesn't speak our tongue, but he makes himself understood. He told they come from a land of snow and ice. I sometimes take whale's teeth from him...they carve easier, but this is finer material. Thank the Lord, there's plenty of call for my work since the abbey opened. When I was a youth, I scraped by making brooches or those who'd pay me in food and drink. I'm my own man nowadays, as are you Master Leather-worker."

"But these tusks don't look anything like what you showed me earlier," I observed.

He laughed and said, "That's because I have to take my small axe to strip away the outer rind. Then, I saw them into sections as needed and take this tool here, it's called a *float*, to pare the surface and only then can I use a gouge and different-sized chisels to work the ivory."

Enthralled, I thanked him and promising to return in a twelvemonth, I left his peaceful haven for the bustle of the street, well aware of what had happened that morning. My senses had been awakened and I had become receptive to the idea of human perception being directed by the correct prompts.

Far better, I thought, to have surrendered to the expert suggestions of the carver than to seek to impose my ideas on him.

Satisfied and cheerful, on impulse, I bought the shawl I'd considered for Sherlaith seven days before. She could wear it when she was feeding our child, I thought happily. I regained my horse, gave the stable lad a silver coin because he'd groomed the beast so well and left Hexham in high spirits, thankful that the sun was yellow and not black.

TWENTY-FOUR

RIDING, NORTHUMBRIA, NOVEMBER 687 AD

THE CHEERLESS GREY OF THE ADVANCING AUTUMN
tended to drive me into an introspective mood, but this year,
with Sherlaith growing more exuberant as her belly swelled, I
remained even-tempered. Only when inspiration evaded me
and I was left staring at the scarce content of Book II did I veer
towards despondency. I desired to produce four books of equal
length and importance, but if I could not remember more of
Cuthbert's time as a monk, what was I to do? I tried
meditation, prayer and self-loathing, none of which had any
effect until I surrendered to acceptance.

Often, I wonder whether I am in control of my actions or
perhaps I should learn, like Job, to accept the life conferred
upon me. I have come to believe that mine is guided by an
unseen force. I hesitate to say that Cuthbert was ensuring the
suitability of my work from beyond the grave but too many
inexplicable occurrences in crucial moments had so far
ensured its continuity.

In the middle of my enforced creative pause, as I glowered

in futile desperation at my quill pen, Sherlaith accompanied a man into the workshop where my father was silently and respectfully going about his work. Instinctively, my parent knew when not to disturb my concentration. We both looked up, probably with the same thought that my wife was showing a new customer into our leather-working sanctuary. This notion was soon refuted when Sherlaith indicated me, and not Oswin, to the newcomer.

"Good morning, Brother Aella—" and this misapprehension alerted me to the nature of our visitor although he wore no habit, "forgive the intrusion. My name is Tydi and I am a priest. In my younger days, I was a monk in the same house as the blessed Cuthbert. I am delighted that the Holy Father has seen fit to canonise him." He paused and stared at the illustration of Cuthbert washing the angel's feet, but did not comment, continuing, "I have come here from Lindisfarena to find you, Brother, where together with many other pilgrims I visited the saint's shrine. Conversing with the monks, I learnt about your work and heard that you seek people who knew Cuthbert. I have some remarkable tales and thought you might like to include them in your tome, which I see is progressing well, the Lord be praised!"

I grabbed his hand and implored him to tell me all he could about my never to be forgotten friend. Sherlaith was more thoughtful and brought food and drink for the weary traveller, which he accepted and devoured whilst I sat there impatiently for him to finish eating.

"I can tell you this first account with complete certainty because I was with him," began the priest encouragingly. "Cuthbert, another brother and myself sailed to the land of the Picts, a place called Niuduera, where we waited without food for the sea to calm so that we could resume our voyage. Our hunger was terrible, I recall to this day, Brother Aella, the pangs of starvation lancing through my belly and how Cuthbert urged us to pray, saying, *God will provide.* And of course, He did. On the beach, we found three slices of prepared dolphin meat, enough to sustain us for three days. What do you think of that?"

"A miracle!" I exclaimed and resolved to include it in Book II, thankful that it would help partly solve my problem of lack of inspiration for that section.

When I and my other companion proclaimed this, as you said, a *miracle,* Cuthbert smiled and said that an angel always provided for him. He went on to tell us about a similar circumstance, but of course, I did not see it with my eyes as I did the account I have just given you."

"Please go on," I pleaded, keen for more material for my book.

"Cuthbert told me that he and a boy were walking along the River Teviot teaching and baptising the mountain people thereabouts when a golden eagle swooped from the sky and landed by the river. The boy ran towards the bird and found a large fish," the priest frowned and in a serious tone said, "I'd guess it would have been a salmon, anyway, the boy took out his seax, divided the fish, giving half to the eagle and he and Cuthbert fed on the other part. I thought you would wish to hear about this happening."

I beamed at the cleric, and in hope asked, "Do you have any more tales of Cuthbert from his time as a monk?"

Tydi's brow wrinkled and he stroked his chin until, after a while, he said, "Well there's Cuthbert and the fire; I heard it from another brother. On the same trip as the eagle episode, the Devil created an illusion of a burning house, tricking some of the men despite Cuthbert's warning; the men afterwards realised their mistake when they sought to extinguish the fire and were forced to beg the saint's forgiveness, which he granted." The priest's countenance suddenly appeared to have had a moment's recollection, "Then, there's what Cuthbert himself recounted to me, I'd almost forgotten, he related how he saved from flames the house of his childhood nanny, a nun and a widow named Kenwith of Hruringaham, through prayer." He paused, appearing deep in thought.

At the same time, I remembered that my friend had told me about his foster mother of that name.

"Even the elements obeyed the Lord through Cuthbert," I mused.

Thanking the pilgrim priest from the depths of my heart, I offered him a bed for the night, but he refused, saying that he had to continue his journey. As soon as he had departed, I picked up my quill and began to recount the story of the dolphin meat. The next day, I added the other tales and sat back to verify that Book II needed little more for it to match Book I for the amount of content.

The question for me now was what to do next. To decide, I wandered to my favourite place for contemplation: Edwy's Cross. The day was dull and chilly, but the cold air helped clear my thoughts. I sat huddled on the usual bole and meditated. After a while, I decided that Book II might be deemed complete, except that it lacked an illustration. I considered the episode of the eagle the most suitable for an image, but there was a problem: I'd never in my life seen an eagle and didn't know what one looked like, which brings me back to the unseen guiding force I mentioned earlier.

A swoosh made me raise my eyes in time to see an enormous tawny-brown bird of prey alight on top of the sandstone cross. *Twee-o!* It called and its beady eye fixed on me, its vicious hooked bill in profile. I noticed the golden feathers along the nape of its neck and realised with a start that this was a golden eagle—a raptor rarely or never seen hereabouts. This was no coincidence! I stared at it taking in every detail of the majestic creature, from its square tail, feathered legs, to its noble head. A barking call and it departed in a noisy flurry to then soar and glide in a circle over me before its powerful wings carried it away north, no doubt to some mountain eyrie.

I dashed back to my workbench, grabbed a brush and some parchment and depicted the hawk I had seen. Satisfied that I'd faithfully captured its likeness, I prepared the surface for the illustration, which now would give me no further difficulty. This time, I created, at first in my mind, a geometric background of reddish-brown with a golden insert. High on a green, grassy bank the eagle perched with its talons sunk into the severed head of the salmon, ripping it with its beak. Below, on one knee, the boy in a red tunic, seax in his right hand was de-scaling the tail end of the fish. Behind the boy, wearing a black habit, staff in his left hand, stood Cuthbert, indicating the fish with his right forefinger extended, advising the boy, who had his head turned receptively towards the monk. The whole I would finish inside the usual narrow, golden frame.

Having conceived the image to my satisfaction, I outlined it lightly in hard charcoal, ready to paint the next day.

"What bird is that, son?"

My father had come to gaze at the painting I'd done from memory.

"It's a golden eagle, Father. It settled on the wayside cross on the road to Corbridge."

"Impossible! Yon's a mountain hawk, we don't get that sort around here. You find them up in Pictland."

"I know that, but I'm telling you, little more than the time it took me to run back here, and I saw it perch on the cross."

My father looked sceptical, rightly so, for had I not seen it, I wouldn't have believed such a yarn, either. But I knew what had happened and whereas I would never have told anyone else, Oswin was my father and I wanted to tell him.

"It's not natural. That bird was sent by God so that I could illustrate Cuthbert's tale. Until I saw it, I didn't know what that hawk looked like. Now, you see how important *our* book is?" I knew he would put his best work into the cover but I wanted him to feel as committed as I did.

"Ay," he said, "It's a miracle and I'll make a start on the binding in the New Year."

I'd explained to him about the roundels and made him a new template. A few days before, I'd caught him practising new scrollwork on an offcut involving the head and legs of a strange biting beast. I pretended not to have noticed but thought it quite splendid.

Talk of the cover reminded me that I had to go up north to Pictland, for only in their rivers could freshwater mussel pearls be found. Or, at least, that is what the ivory carver had told me. He said they came in a range of shapes and colours but that the most desirable hue was pastel pink. That would also blend beautifully with our tinted leather.

The off-putting journey north could be made more bearable by ship, but not until the spring came because a winter voyage on the storm-tossed sea was likely to end one's life by drowning. The roads were already becoming impassable. Luckily, I still had Books III and IV to produce. The purchase of pearls could wait. Sherlaith, never slow to voice an opinion, declared that silver-white pearls were much nicer than pastel pink ones. Given her infallible good taste, I decided to see what was available and what prices might be asked—not that I could afford to be niggardly and skimp over the king's cover.

Setting aside my work for the day, I went indoors to persuade Sherlaith to come for a walk, figuring that the air would do her and the child in her womb the world of good.

"Let's pay a call on Nerian and Eawynn," I suggested.

"We'll take them some of my honey cake," she chirped.

On the way, I told her about the golden eagle I'd seen.

"It's just a large buzzard," she teased, unimpressed until I explained what lay behind its appearance.

"I think an angel must have carried it south on its arm and then sent it to Edwy's Cross."

Now I didn't know if she was teasing or being serious because Sherlaith was as mischievous as she was religious. She knelt by the bed to say her prayers every night without fail. I glanced sideways at her solemn face and opted for the latter.

In the mill house, I wondered why Eawynn was so brusque in her greeting and why then she dragged Sherlaith apart to whisper some guarded secret. I was still exchanging pleasantries with Nerian when my wife burst out, exuberant as ever,

"If you don't tell him, I swear I'll blurt it right now!"

Eawynn looked stricken, and in a tiny voice said,

"Nerian, you're going to be a father!"

The relief on her face to have shared her news with her husband was plain to see. I wondered why then she hadn't spoken of it. Women were a mystery to me.

He bounded to her and enfolded her close to his chest, exchanged a few low words that I didn't hear and kissed her repeatedly before turning, grinning at me and saying,

"They'll be playmates and I'll call him, Aella!"

I feigned a serious expression, "Easy, my friend, it might be a girl."

He frowned, then laughed, "Ah, in that case, they'll wed!"

Sherlaith's tinkling laugh gained our attention,

"And ours might be a girl, too."

Now Nerian bellowed with laughter, I saw that he was mad with joy,

"Then I was right in the first place! They'll be playmates!"

My wife giggled again, "In which case, you'll call her Ser-la..."

Nerian looked anguished, "Don't be offended, Ser-la, but I can't. If it's a girl. I'll name her after mother."

"Osythe is a fine name," I beamed, looking anxiously at Sherlaith.

"And, so it is!" said my delightful wife with the sweetest of smiles.

Back home, she looked at me lovingly.

"If Eawynn's calculations are correct, her babe will be born in May, so there'll only be four months between them. They're sure to be fast friends, whatever their sex."

"Ay, it's a splendid day for us all! Osythe is sure to be overjoyed."

"Pah! What sort of a name's *Osythe?* Ser-la's much prettier."

"Ser-la's a good name for a wildcat."

She rushed at me, snatching a knife from the table. I dodged out of the door calling back,

"Take care, feral beast, or your babe will be an orphan!"

I sat down in the workshop and stared blankly at the parchment, for the hundredth time counting back the months to our babe's conception. No matter how hard I tried, I couldn't make the birth come at Christ's Mass. The date remained steadfastly in February. By then, I hoped to have Book III written and maybe I'd wait till after Eawynn's babe saw the light before travelling to Pictland. I had meant to ask Nerian to come with me but hadn't wanted to trespass on his moment of joy. I would ask him soon though.

Right now, I had to concentrate on my illustration after having disturbed the celestial powers for the glimpse of the golden eagle.

TWENTY-FIVE

RIDING, NORTHUMBRIA, WINTER 687-8 AD

CHRIST'S MASS PASSED WITH MOST OF THE VILLAGERS uniting in festivities and since it had been a year of plenty, and the weather unseasonably mild, there was much merriment. The occasion enabled me to broach the journey into Pictland with Nerian. Miscalculating, I thought he'd be more persuadable with ale inside him. Understandably, he was hesitant, owing to Eawynn's condition. When I told him I was prepared to put back departure until after the birth of his babe, I won him round but not without some difficulty.

I explained, thus, what the voyage would entail,

"We'll take out a small boat from nearby with three crewmen and sail northwards to Pictland, constantly staying within sight of the coast, until we come to the estuary known as Ythan. My friend, the ivory carver, told me the best pearls are found in that river. To find it, we'll direct our course to a place, excuse my pronunciation," I hesitated and tried hard, "called *Fearann Mhàrtainn...*" Nerian laughed and swigged more ale, "It means *Martin's Land* in the Pictish tongue."

"Why didn't you say so right away?"

I scowled at him; maybe he'd had too much to drink. He hiccoughed and I knew my impression was correct.

"Is this *Martin's* place near where our Edwy died?"

I frowned, knowing it was not.

"No, that's farther north and inland."

"Hic! I want to go there."

"Well, you can't!"

He glared and I had a sinking feeling.

"Whatdy mean?" his voice was slurred, "I'm coming alldway up there—"

I used my cunning.

"Let's talk about it another time, Nerian, I've had too much to drink to think straight."

He couldn't pick a fight if I accused myself. So, I decided to let the matter lie until the spring, nearer the time of his child's birth. Anyway, I'd already obtained his promise to sail north with me.

Meanwhile, having long concluded Book II, I made a solid start on the third part: about Cuthbert's time as an island hermit. I remember well how he told me about his solitary existence on Farne.

I closed my eyes with my quill still poised over the parchment and recalled the conversation,

"Aella, my purpose of retreating to the island was for the sake of the sweetness of divine contemplation. Our Lord declared *Blessed are the pure in heart, for they shall see God* — that is what I yearned to do. To achieve such a state of grace, I had to strip off all that bound me to the outside world. Understand, my friend that there is an unseen war..." He paused, I remember, entering one of those trance-like moments that transported him far away. Reconnecting, he said,

"I chose the island because it is farther into the ocean and, so, more open to the wildness of the sea and the wind and thus,

Aella, more conducive to contemplation. It is less rugged, for there is some soil to grow crops, but it was a place dense with demons. The hermit, my friend, must be a soldier in the war against the forces of spiritual evil." I shall never forget his next words, "My weapons are prayer and fasting and trust in God." He looked at me with an expression of such intense devotion that I felt compelled to embrace him but that would have missed the point. He continued, "It is in stillness and aloneness that the battle may be won and it is there you must go, my friend, if you wish to grow in God's presence."

Some of this I tried to write in the introduction to my Book III, but I found it easier to recount how Cuthbert set about constructing his hermitage. He needed to move a massive rock to continue with his building and being too feeble, resorted to prayer and woke to find it gone. An oratory and a cell, he built, surrounding both with a wall so high it shut out all save the heavens above. Some men accompanied him to help him in this laborious task and one morning, he took them to a spot nearby and asked them to dig up some stony ground—thankless work, which they obediently set about—where, suddenly, a spring spouted forth giving an endless supply of fresh water. Cuthbert told me that to complete the roof of his cell, a twelve-foot beam served but his men could not find one, so after some days of patiently waiting in vain, he settled on prayer for a solution. The sea obliged and the waves provided him with the beam he needed.

I was able to finish this account in January and by now, Sherlaith was well advanced and heavy with child. My excitement grew as we entered February. The weather in this month is often variable in Riding. Impatiently I waited as the rainy, grey days slipped by and still my babe, perhaps not wishing to risk the inclement clime clung stubbornly within the womb. I can remember as if yesterday, how the weather behaved before my firstborn's arrival. The month neared its end and, on the 25th, it was cold, cloudy and damp from the preceding rain and snow. The next night, there was quite a frost, but in the day, it melted by itself, without rain. On the 26th and the following night there was a great wind but much snow, and on the 27th it kept snowing till vespers. The day after, at about the third hour, it again began to snow heavily, which was when little Edwy arrived, kicking and bawling, into the white-blanketed world. I often wonder whether children born in a snowstorm are tougher than others. Certainly, my Edwy grew strong and formidable but I'm getting way ahead of myself.

I did little work on the king's book in March, being too taken with my newborn son and with looking after his weakened mother as well as I could. Sherlaith recovered and after five weeks was back to her energetic, mischievous self. She adored her child and our life was blessed with great happiness. Soon, it would be time for Eawynn to present Nerian with a babe. Midway through March, I went to the mill to check on them and to be sure Nerian had not changed his mind about accompanying me in May.

"I gave you my word and there's no reason to change it," his tone was sullen.

"We can set off a score of days after the birth, by then Eawynn will be stronger and Osythe will help with the chores."

Nerian looked edgy, his expression defensive,

"Why did you say we couldn't go to the place where Edwy died?"

I frowned, *not that again!*

"I can understand your desire, Nerian, Edwy was my best friend, but it's impossible."

"Why?"

"For one thing, it's much farther north and inland. It'd take us months to get there and back. I don't know about you, but I won't want to be away from my babe all that time. Second, and not least, the Picts are a wild, savage folk and we'd be risking staying with your brother forever if you take my meaning."

He nodded reluctantly and my heart went out to him. I laid a hand on his shoulder,

"It's because I don't trust the Picts that I'm taking you with me, Nerian, you'll cover my back like Edwy did for me in the old days."

"I don't have a weapon other than my seax."

"I'll ask my father to lend you his sword; he fought the Mercians before I was born and it's a fine blade."

Taking my leave, I returned, heartened, to the workshop and arranged for the loan of Oswin's sword. At first, the old warrior was reluctant to part with it even for a while. He kept it hanging in its sheath on the wall nearest his workbench and occasionally he would draw it to lovingly to oil the blade and swing the weapon as in his youth. When he understood that the two of us were to venture into hostile territory in another two moons, he agreed to my request.

Those weeks went by quickly since I had little Edwy to occupy my time when not poring over my writing. The babe was growing healthily and found comfort in my arms when the cholic made him yowl. My calmness settled him, surely not my singing! I loved it when he twined my beard in those delightful minuscule fingers, although he sometimes made my eyes water when he tugged too hard.

On the second day of May, Nerian burst into our workshop.

From the joy on his face, I knew at once that his child was born.

"It's a girl, Aella! My little Osythe's seen the light! I swear she's the prettiest creature in Northumbria! Will you come? Bring Sherlaith, Eawynn will be pleased to see her."

Of course, I accepted eagerly, but in my heart, I was disappointed. I had wanted it to be a boy bearing my name and a sturdy playmate in the future for Edwy. But our wyrd is strangely woven and unbeknown to either of us in that joyous moment, Nerian had predicted their fate months before. As if sealing a pact with destiny, Sherlaith brought little Edwy to the mill to greet Osythe. Already friends, the two mothers became inseparable companions from that day forth, taking it in turns to exchange visits as soon as Eawynn had regained her strength.

Three weeks later, I knocked on the mill house door and thrust the sheathed sword into Nerian's hand. He strapped it around his waist, picked up his pack and told me to wait at the gate whilst he took his leave. I caught a glimpse of Eawynn's pale and anxious face at the door and felt guilty at taking her husband on a long and potentially dangerous journey. In the days leading up to our departure, Nerian had worked the mill for long hours, building up a stock of flour for his mother to sell in his absence so that they would not lose loyal customers.

We reached the coast before midday and, spurning food, I sought a shipowner and his two brothers who I had befriended on one of my previous visits to Lindisfarena. This man was a local fisherman who had bemoaned the difficulty of supporting a wife, children and two siblings with one vessel. That was why I was sure I could persuade him to take us outside the waters he knew so well, much farther north. Money was no obstacle for me, given the king's generosity. I found my skipper on board his ship, tending to his nets.

"Hail, friend!" I called, "Good catch today?"

"Not so much as a sniff of herring," he said, "It's as if they've upped and crossed the sea to fill the Frisians' nets."

I'd never heard of Frisians before but from his words, I deduced they lived way across the North Sea.

"So, you'll be a bit short of earnings, Master Fisherman."

"Ay, times are hard," he scowled, his weather-beaten face looking fierce, "but what's it to you?"

I grinned and said, "May I come aboard with my friend? We have an offer for you."

His interest was piqued, "Ay, but watch your step, it's slippy, I haven't had time to sluice the boards yet."

We boarded without mishap and I offered my hand, which he clasped.

"I know your face," he frowned trying to remember.

"Aella. We met more than a twelvemonth ago, you told me when to cross to the isle."

"Ay, so I did. So, what's this offer then?"

"I want you and your brothers to take us north to a port in the Pictish lands. We'll stay to conclude a purchase and then turn around and come back. I'll pay you well," I added hastily.

He looked askance and went back to picking at his net.

Nerian and I exchanged a worried glance before I tried again,

"Don't you wish to earn a tidy sum, Master Fisherman?"

His expression was sullen, not to say uncooperative,

"That's a good two-days' sailing if the wind's favourable and more if it ain't. Those are unfamiliar waters and all, then, there are my brothers to pay and then there's the journey back. It'd cost you more than you can scrape together, Master Leather-worker—that's right ain't it?"

"Ay, I'm a leather-worker, your memory serves you well, but that isn't to say I can't meet your price; I'm on the king's business."

I saw the flash of interest in his eyes and he frowned and pondered,

"Given all the circ'stances, I'd say it'll cost you twenty sceattas, my friend."

I laughed and slapped Nerian on the back,

"That's fair enough, but I'll tell you what, I'll give you twenty, here and now, and the same sum when we've returned here."

The fisherman gawped and looked out to sea.

"The weather's set fine and we can sail on the morning tide at dawn, it'll be running right. Now, what about the twenty sceattas? I groped inside my tunic and selected the correct money bag. I had three, keeping the gold separate. Shaking out coins into my palm, I counted: "...eighteen-nineteen- twenty!"

He noted there was still money in the bag but he could also see the axe slung across my shoulder and Nerian's sword—not that I had reason to doubt his honesty.

"What about an inn for the night?"

He stood, tossed the net in the bows and said,

"You'll eat with us tonight, but for now, I'll take you to my cousin's tavern. He does a good fish pie and I'll see you get clean bedding for the night."

This was a splendid arrangement that turned out satisfactorily in every way. We only needed to sleep till dawn and then we'd be away to sea.

TWENTY-SIX

IN TURNS, ONE OF THE FISHERMEN BROTHERS KEPT A vigilant eye on the sea from the prow as any distraction could lead to wrecking on a submerged rock. This was always a risk when following along and keeping close to the coast. We had no map to guide us with landmarks to ascertain our progress. I had only the ivory carver's words for directions.

"Sail north, past the wide estuary, carry on beyond the first large bay, then there's a settlement named *Obar Dheathain* with two estuaries, the second is a fishers' hamlet. If you are unsure, you should put in there and ask but once that harbour is at your backs, there is a long beach until the mouth of the Ythan. If you come to the rugged cliffs, you have gone too far and must turn back."

These instructions oriented us so well, thanks also to the clear weather, that we didn't lose our bearings and late on the second day tied up in *Fearann Mhàrtainn*, our destination. Since daylight was fading, we did not disembark but opted to spend the night aboard, wrapped in our cloaks. I took the first watch and woke Nerian after three hours according to my calculation using the Lodestar, as my father had taught me. My friend was supposed to wake me after another three hours, but our skipper stopped him from doing so, kindly taking the lookout himself.

When daylight was broad enough for us to disembark and find local fishermen to talk to, we encountered a seemingly insuperable problem. These wiry, dark-haired Picts could not understand our language, nor we theirs. At last, I found one patient enough to struggle with sign language and try to comprehend my needs. I used a broken mussel shell from the quay and by gestures pointed inside it and made a circular motion to suggest a pearl. He was a sharp-witted youth and understood me. I pressed a sceat into his hand and flicked my fingers four times to indicate a score of pearls. Pulling at my arm, he led me along the estuary to a wooden hut. Wicker baskets hung on nails banged into the walls either side of the door. The lad knocked and another wiry character with streaks of grey in his hair came out.

My guide spoke rapidly and held up the silver coin I had given him, then started with another flood of words. I noticed the hut owner's eyes gaze over my shoulder and half-turning was happy to see that Nerian had followed us discreetly this far. I raised both hands up and flicked the fingers once. By this, I meant a score of pearls. The interpreter spoke again and the fellow disappeared indoors, returning with three pearls. One was rose pink, another silver white and the third salmon-coloured. I didn't need the youth to explain that I was being given a choice of colour. I pointed to the pink pearl. I loved the delicate hue. The trader grinned, showing a set of rotten teeth and re-entered his dwelling.

Movement caught my eyes and it appeared we had company. Five Picts had gathered at a dozen paces from us, their attitude seemed one of curiosity, so I relaxed and smiled but that elicited no positive reaction.

The pearl man came out holding a pouch. Standing close to me, he removed a palmful of the variously-shaped pearls. I noticed at once that no two were identical and this added to their charm. I longed to strike a deal. Again, with my hand, I indicated twenty. The fellow looked shrewdly, shook his head and my heart sank. I was so near to getting what I'd come for only to have it refused! But I had misunderstood. It wasn't that he didn't want to part with the pearls, on the contrary, the rascal wanted to sell the pouchful—to make more money.

I scrabbled inside my tunic and took out the money bag of silver sceattas, showing him one and asking with an exaggerated expression how much he wanted. The old fox took a sceat, frowned gave it back, spat on the ground and shook his head. I knew what that meant. I tucked away the silver and pulled out another purse. There's a very old saying,

He fishes well who uses a golden hook.

I took out a gold coin and handed it to the scoundrel. He bit it and grinned, sticking up two fingers. I sighed and handed over another coin. That was the moment I realised that our transaction, or rather the sight of gold, was causing a commotion among the five onlookers. Hurriedly, I thrust my purse back inside my tunic along with the pouch of pearls. Just the time to clasp the pearl man's hand to acknowledge our deal and I strode over to Nerian,

"Let's get out of here, I don't like the look of those villains."

I was right, too, even as I spoke, Nerian saved me by pushing me off balance so that a sharp stone from a sling whistled harmlessly past my head. We unslung our shields, drew our weapons and charged the attackers. This was not the best strategy, because they vanished into the landscape and more stones winged through the air, but we parried them and no harm came to us.

"Run," I yelled and we dashed away, following the path we had taken before. I hadn't gone more than fifty paces when I felt a crippling pain behind my thigh: I could run no more.

"Wait, Nerian! I've been hit! I can't run—" in truth, I could only limp or hobble. Luckily, our stout fishermen friends had seen us fleeing and were coming to our aid. Now the odds were balanced and the Picts remained out of sight although their stones whizzed through the air, too close for comfort.

"Come, Aella, throw your arm about me," cried the skipper and half-limping, half-dragged, I made it to the quay and on-board the blessed boat. "Cast off!" he yelled and within moments our vessel was being rowed away from the hostile shore.

"Treacherous bastards!" Nerian growled, and then he said something that pleased me, "You were right, Aella, it is as well we didn't venture out in search of Edwy's grave. We'd never have survived that journey if this is ought to go by. To our relief, the sail went up, filled and we cut out into the sea. I was too busy exploring my bruised and tender thigh to look back, but one of the brothers averted our skipper.

There's a ship coming after us, by the look of it!"

We all stared back and it was true, a sail was being raised and I thought I could see one of the crew with a handful of javelins.

"We have a fair wind," our skipper proclaimed, "and by the look of the lines of that tub, we're the hare and yon's the weasel!"

I wasn't quite sure what he meant by that and asked.

"Does that mean we can sail faster than them?"

"Have you never seen a weasel chase a hare?"

I shook my head and lost patience.

"I ain't. Just answer the question!"

He gave me a sour look and growled,

"Ay, well, we'll soon leave them behind, you'll see."

They were persistent, but the skipper knew about ships and he was right, our sleeker hull and larger sail made the difference. The Picts couldn't get close enough to hurl a javelin or to sling a stone, which was fortunate, such was the skill they possessed with that weapon, as my throbbing thigh proved. After an hour or thereabouts, the small shape behind us disappeared from view.

I turned to Nerian, and shared my concern,

"Let's hope we don't have to put in along this shore, given their notion of hospitality—pray the fine weather holds."

An anguished thought occurred to me. The presence of the hostile Picts during the transaction had made me careless. I had assumed that the pouch was full of pearls, but for all I knew, they might have been apple pips. I sat on a coiled rope, spread a cloth over my lap and poured the contents of the pouch onto it. Thankfully, the lustrous pink pearls shone in the sunlight and I laughed with relief. We could hardly have gone back to argue the matter if the Pict had swindled me—he probably had, anyway, because while the pearls likely were worth one gold piece, two of the coins seemed outrageous. Still, the money was King Aldfrith's and the finished binding would be so beautiful that the expense, however extortionate, would be justifiable. I sincerely hoped never more to encounter a Pict, but luckily for my peace of mind, I was no seer and did not fear the future.

Back in Babbanburgh, the fisherman's wife, apart from being an excellent cook, was skilled in herbal cures. When she saw me limp into their house, she had me remove my leggings.

"That's a vile bruise, Master Aella, what's needed is wolfsbane." She hurried to fetch a small pot of ointment. "Not that you'll be sampling this, but you should know it's poisonous, and there's nought like it for soothing and removing bruises." She had me lie prone on a litter and began to work the unguent into the back of my thigh.

"The swine wanted to bring me down to rob me of my coin," I muttered through clenched teeth. "Your husband helped me flee. He's more than earned his pay."

"My Esa's a good man and a fine sailor."

I had to agree with that and on impulse reached into my tunic, took out two sceattas and two pink pearls.

"You take these to a gem-worker, Mistress, and have him make you a brooch. It's my gift to you."

Her face turned a charming shade of pink and she grinned,

"Thank you. You will eat with us since it's late and you need to rest that leg at least tonight.

"Nerian, go to the inn and have a room made up for us and while you're about it bring two flagons of ale back with you."

When the door closed, I asked, "What is this wolfsbane, Mistress?"

"I make it up with the petals, Master Aella, it's a violet-blue flower and grows on mountain meadows."

"But there are no mountains hereabouts."

She giggled, "Ay, it's true. These came from the north: the Pictish lands."

I growled, "Well, there's a fine thing! It takes a Pictish plant to cure a Pictish bruise."

We both laughed and Esa joined in, adding, "If Master Aella had a Pict here now, I wager he'd make the villain sample your ointment spread on bread, wife."

"Well I wouldn't offer him ale from Nerian's flagon, that's for sure— if ever the laggard gets here."

We laughed again, but the Picts were a sore point for me in more than one sense. I picked up Esa's daughter, a five-year-old, and sat her on my knee, to her delight showing her tricks with a coin. Her squeals of pleasure made me think two things: I could not wait for Edwy to be old enough to display such tricks for him and how it might be a splendid idea to have a daughter of my own.

That was the moment when the father of a newborn daughter walked in carrying two welcome flagons of ale to begin our convivial evening across the causeway from Lindisfarena— the almost forgotten reason for our presence there.

TWENTY-SEVEN

RIDING, NORTHUMBRIA, 688-90 AD

Life settled into a routine of writing, illustrating and family life after my return from Pictland. My father, in his inimitable patient style of working, began poring over the cover of the *Vita Sancti Cuthberti*. The crimson goat leather made an excellent backdrop for the rose-pink freshwater pearls I had procured and the petal-form frame destined to house the ivory plaque of Christ in Majesty was bewitchingly attractive.

The brief journey to Hexham and the carver's fee paid, saw me return with a box stuffed with linen packets to protect the intricate work of the master craftsman, who had produced plaques in relief worthy of our king. My father was so in awe that he told me,

"Aella, I have the clumsy hands of an old man," which was untrue because no youth could have been steadier or more precise, "I fear to damage these delicate carvings. You must insert them into their leather housings."

He prepared the glue himself to a recipe that would ensure no staining and I, perhaps having absorbed his trepidation, completed the insertions without blemish but with tension to the muscles my neck that took a day to shake off.

Together we admired his handiwork and despite the magnificence of the binding, which with the insertion of the rubies would be a masterpiece, we both knew that there was still one last bridge to cross. The stitching and glueing of the gathered pages into the cover. I embraced my father and said,

"Father, as a teacher and craftsman you have no equal, set aside your binding as best you think fit to protect it from the air and grime, for ahead of me, await two years of toil to finish the book."

"Two years!" he laughed, "This Cuthbert of yours must have been a remarkable fellow. I wish I could read what you tell about him. If you wrote my story, Aella, it would be finished in two pages."

He saw my eye stray to his sword hanging on the wall,

"Oh, ay, I was forgetting, the Mercian campaign!" and he started one of his rambling recollections. "The disgrace of it! Losing the battle at the Trent—it was a long, hard-fought affair and many a good man forsook this life beside that river..." and so he went on and I listened, as ever, with interest although I'd heard it many times before.

Will I relate our defeat in Pictland to Edwy when my hair is grey?

My father returned to the daily labour of leather-working and the monotony of my writing and drawing was interrupted occasionally by the welcome appearance of a villager to collect or order work. Otherwise, the seasons came and went and Edwy grew stronger and more mischievous like his mother until one day, the most unexpected visit occurred. As usual, I was perfecting my uncial letters with wedge-shaped finials as I had been taught at Lismore Abbey when Sherlaith burst into the workshop with a grin as wide as her slender waist.

"You'll never guess!" she cried, bouncing from one foot to the other in such a state of excitement that I lay my pen beside my work and stood.

"That is as certain as the sun rising in the east!"

"Oh, Aella!" she threw herself into my arms, "They have come from Ardfinnan!"

I pushed her roughly from me and ran out of the workshop, almost colliding with Lugaid holding a giggling Edwy close to his chest, legs dangling.

"Brother, have a care! Would you harm the brightest man in the family?"

I believe he was referring to Edwy and not himself, but in either case, it was banter spoken to mock me. But never was jesting more welcome. I hurried to find Sherlaith's parents with my mother, enjoying her famed honey cake. This was the beginning of a week of merrymaking, in which somehow, we managed to involve the whole village. I believe there was not a single villager who did not warm to the gigantic auburn-haired and -bearded Uá Broíthe chieftain, who surpassed us all in the art of revelry. The days flew by and I cannot say who among the two families was the most sorrowful at their departure. Sherlaith's father tried every form of enticement to have us transfer to Ériu but the pressing need to finish King Aldfrith's commission made me refute his beguiling offer of land. Goodness knows I was tempted, not least by the extraordinary friendship with Lugaid, so dear to me.

Soon after their departure, I concluded Book III with the singular account of Cuthbert and the ravens. This surely was the most curious of the episodes that Cuthbert had related to me. So strange did I find it that I decided to illustrate it, too. On Farne, the hermit had constructed a refuge for those monks who insisted on serving him. I recall his words, "Aella, I warned those ravens more than once not to settle on the roof of the shelter and disturb my servants. But would they heed me? They would not! At last, by their persistence, they forced me to banish them from the island in the name of Jesus." I still remember his happy and triumphant smile as he announced, "after three days one raven returned seeking pardon and, of course, I forgave it, so it came back again with one of its fellows bearing enough pig lard to grease everyone's boots for a whole year." I had to agree with my friend that this was an amazing occurrence and having written it in the book, I added a painting of the shelter with four ravens on the roof and one at the feet of the hermit, presenting him a wodge of pig lard.

I felt sure that there were enough accounts in this part and eager to proceed to the fourth and final book, I closed the third with a summary of the saint's virtues and achievements.

Book IV was the most problematical for me because it covered the period after my departure for Ériu, and after they had prevailed on Cuthbert to become bishop of Lindisfarena—the post he held when I knew him. Therefore, much of the content dealt with the last years of his life and miracles occurring after his death. As I have mentioned, some kindly and willing monks, like Baldhelm, had provided me with material, but aware of the shortcomings in terms of quantity, I resolved to return to Lindisfarena in the summer to see whether I might garner more tales. I decided to take the first three books to show him my progress.

Before my departure, I wrote the account given to me by Baldhelm about the healing of the Tweedside gesith, or retainer of King Ecgfrith. His master, Sibba, distressed by the illness of his faithful servant and moved by the anguish of the man's wife, came with all haste to ask for Cuthbert's help. Baldhelm explained thus,

"Cuthbert ordered a monk to fetch a dish of water, raised a hand in blessing and instructed him to give it to another of

Sibba's servants and take it to the priest attending the stricken man. This he did and, Aella, that cleric sprinkled the blessed water on the invalid, who recovered his health to the joy of his wife and all others present."

I wrote this faithfully but decided the tale did not warrant an illustration.

When I had made sure the ink was dry, I gathered this page together with the rest, packed my bag and walked to the coast. I visited my fisherman friend and was pleased to see his wife wearing a delightful brooch displaying the river pearls I'd given her.

On the island, I at once sought audience with the abbot who, delighted with my achievements, grew concerned at my worries about content for the last book. He frowned and berated himself for struggling to recall names, blaming it on his age.

"Come back later, Aella, after Sext; I'm sure to have remembered by then."

When I went back, he beamed, delighted at his successful feat of memory.

"I'm afraid you'll have to undertake a journey, Aella. There was a priest here by the name of Aethilwald and he witnessed a miracle performed by the blessed Cuthbert. At present, he holds the position of prior of Melrose. It is ten and four leagues to the west but I will arrange for you to take one of the abbey horses—you must return it, of course." The abbot went on to recount some miracles that were spoken about on the island but without first-hand accounts and although I made notes, I was unsure about including them in my book. For this reason, I selected carefully and put a mark in my jottings next to the curing of a paralytic boy brought to Cuthbert in the district of Ahse in the mountains between Hexham and Carlisle.

The kindly abbot sent a deferential monk named Tydi to

my quarters with the testimony of a miracle he had witnessed, in which Cuthbert saved an infant and his family from the plague at a village called Medilwong. The monk said, in awestruck tones, "...and he did this by the sole power of faith and prayer, Aella. I touched the flesh where the swellings had been with my hands and watched the fever and disease vanish before me. Only a saint could have intervened with God in that way." He made the sign of the cross and added, "You will include this in your book, won't you?" I gave him my word that I would.

The horse was a fine beast and must have cost the abbey a vast sum, no wonder the abbot insisted on its return. Its powerful muscles made light work of the leagues and I made sure to stop at midday with the sun high overhead to have him rubbed down, watered and fed at a hostelry, where I too refreshed myself.

How pleasant after lunch to be greeted by a whinny and a nuzzle by the handsome black steed. I mounted him and set off at a brisk pace, following a ridgeway before the road dropped down into woodland. I am forever on my guard in unknown woods and with good reason. There, three rogues sprang out of the undergrowth, startling my mount. This was the undoing of one of them because my noble beast reared, almost unsaddling me but I clung on whilst a metal-shod hoof smashed the skull of one of the villains, ending his days as an outlaw. By now with my axe at the ready, I swung at a hand grabbing at my reins and clove it deep to the bone. The scoundrel screamed and ran into the foliage whence he had come, clutching his bleeding arm. The third lost courage and fled for cover whilst I urged my horse into a gallop away along the path we were taking. All the while I blessed my good fortune that the outlaws were not armed with bows and arrows, for I would have had no escape from a silent shaft powered by surprise by an archer hidden among the leaves.

Is it just luck or is it my guardian, Cuthbert?

Before nightfall, I reached Melrose Abbey, located charmingly in a bend of the broad River Tweed, where, once admitted, I entrusted my four-legged saviour and friend to a monk in charge of the stables.

As soon as the prior heard of my errand, he hurried to greet me and considerately insisted that I ate and drank in the refectory before having me escorted to his quarters.

His thin, lined face creased into a broad smile as he offered me a chair,

"Ay, Brother," he began, ignoring my lack of a tonsure, but repeating the forgivable mistake of others as usually only monks were scribes, "I have much fondness for the memory of Cuthbert and still owe him a great debt."

He paused and looked at me as if wishing to evoke the question; I obliged.

"How so, Prior Aethilwald?"

He sat on a wooden chest in the corner of the room in the absence of another chair,

"At the time, I was a monk at Lindisfarena and had agreed to accompany Bishop Cuthbert into the countryside on one of his missions to preach and baptise in remoter places. I think it was no coincidence that my..." he paused and looked embarrassed, "... *selfish* desire to steer the bishop towards my native village of Bedesfeld, but more the mysterious workings of the Holy Spirit. When we arrived among the houses, we were greeted by a distressed youth who, seeing our tonsures, found the hope and courage to plead with us. 'Brothers,' he cried, 'I beg you, come and pray for my sister, she is but a maid and dying of the strangulation disease.' The lad, Aella, had not recognised me and my heart was sorrowful for the pretty young maid who was my also cousin. As you know, that malady blocks the back of the throat as if there was a layer of leather and few survive it. But we hurried to her bedside, where we found her with a ghastly pallor, rasping for breath, but Cuthbert took her hand in his, knelt by her bed and began to pray." The prior fell silent as though lost in memory, but then with an earnest expression, said, "I swear to you, Brother, as the Lord is my witness, the colour returned to my cousin's cheeks and her breathing became normal. Before Cuthbert released her hand, she smiled at us and sat up in bed, declaring herself well. The Lord be praised, to this day she enjoys good health and only thanks to the holy man I am proud to say was my teacher. Will you include this in your book, Brother Aella?"

"I will indeed, Prior, and I thank you for your valuable contribution. The world must know of Cuthbert's prodigies."

I stayed the night in the abbey and left early with the prior's blessings to speed me on my way. I rode un-accosted through the woods where I'd previously met trouble and arrived back safely on Lindisfarena. Parting with the horse was a wrench because I'd formed a strong attachment in a short time. I reclaimed the pages I'd left with the abbot, who had remembered how Cuthbert had cured a monk called Walhstod from dysentery and this brother was still in the monastery. I did not think it necessary to speak with him, but made note of his name and left Lindisfarena with enough material to finish Book IV, especially because the island was alive with the news of miracles that had happened at Cuthbert's shrine.

These were the most important that I re-read from my notes once back in my workshop—exactly as I jotted them down on Lindisfarena and which I would later include in my opus, I quote:

Note 1) 'Holy water from the trench Cuthbert's body had been washed in, cured a boy of demonic possession.

Note 2) A monk from the household of Bishop Willibrord, visiting Lindisfarena, was taken by serious illness but was cured after praying at Cuthbert's coffin.

Note 3) A paralytic youth brought to the island by another monastery for attention from the Lindisfarena infirmarian, was cured only after wearing the shoes once worn by Cuthbert.

Each of these I would include in Book IV after elaborating them and making them more interesting for the reader. Including two illustrations, the accounts I now had to write would take me until the end of the year, so I settled down to months of hard work.

Just before Christ's Mass in the year of Our Lord, 690, I took the last parchment page and gathered it with the rest of Book IV for stitching. My father gently removed the leather cover from its storage and laid it on my workbench in the clear space I'd prepared. He stood by apprehensively, ready to offer advice if needed but reminiscent of what I'd done with Cuthbert's Gospel, I expertly joined all four books with thicker thread inside the binding and glued them in place. At last, years of work lay before us, missing only the four rubies in the king's possession. Inserting those in his presence would be only a matter of minutes and then I would pronounce the completion of the *Vita Sancti Cuthberti*.

TWENTY-EIGHT

RIDING AND ÉRIU, 691-704 AD

The delay in my departure to Babbanburgh until the spring was occasioned more by my fear of the king's reaction to the quality of my work than waiting for the dry weather of May. Bearing my precious package, I gained immediate access to King Aldfrith's presence.

"In Heaven's Name, Master Aella, you have made me bide my time long enough for this moment," his piercing blue eyes held mine, "I hope it has been worthwhile."

With trembling hand, I unwrapped the clean linen from the book to reveal the magnificent binding. And yet, the four vacant holes were an affront to my eye. The king picked up on them at once.

"These cavities are for my rubies, are they not, Master?"

"Sire, they are."

"Then what say you, shall we repair to my chamber and complete your glorious work?"

He smiled at my palpable relief for his praise.

"Come now, surely you were not a-feared that it would not please me?"

The king led me to where no man goes freely and, overawed, I studied the luxurious surroundings: silk drapes, an enormous bed with soft down-filled covers, and of more immediate interest, a steel-banded chest with a series of locks. The monarch produced a ring of keys and dextrously used a sequence to unlock the strongbox. While he groped around inside, he spoke over his shoulder,

"Lay the volume on the bed, Master Aella, or is the covering too soft for you to work on?"

I put my pack on the floor by the bed and placed the book as commanded.

"The task is delicate, Sire, so the bed is perfect."

The king straightened and guffawed,

"Ha-ha! It's a couch designed for soft *flesh!*"

Embarrassed, I rummaged in my backpack and took out a small pot and brush. Feeling the need to explain the intrusion of craft materials among such finery, I said,

"This, sire, is a glue made by my father to a secret mixture. I will hold the gems for an eternity."

The king unlaced and shook the pouch in his hand, causing a cascade of sparkling red to fall onto the bedcover.

"Select four, nay, five—one as a gift for your father."

I gasped my thanks and was careful not to take the largest, but one equal to the others chosen.

"I am rarely mistaken about a man's character, Aella," was his graceful comment.

Dabbing a precise amount of glue into the first hole, I levered the first gem into position with a flat-bladed chisel and secured the jewel with gentle manipulation. Already with one ruby positioned, the cover assumed a vital magnificence bestowed by the glistening, fiery gem. With the fourth in place, the effect was one of overwhelming beauty as the eye passed in progression from one ivory plaque to the next just as the carver had promised.

"And this is our beloved Cuthbert!" cried King Aldfrith, pointing to the disc in the bottom right-hand corner.

I felt it wiser to say nothing but watched joyfully as my king turned to the title page and read aloud,

"Vita Sancti Cuthberti."

With those words pronounced by the royal tongue, at last, I felt my work had ended.

"You have become erudite, Master Aella. What will you do now?"

"Sire, I have been granted land in Ériu, I seek your permission to take my family to my wife's homeland."

I swear the king looked sorrowful for a fleeting moment. But graciously, he said,

"After your creation," he indicated the book, "I must accord you your heart's desire. But, Aella, there is a condition, how old is your son?"

This surprised and worried me at the same time.

"My Lord, he has but four winters to his name."

The king smiled, "Enjoy his infancy, Aella, but give me your word that when he reaches ten and four that you will send him into my service if God grants me long life."

"I'm sure He will, Sire, and I swear it."

The king gave me his hand—the first and last time I have touched royal flesh. So, the fateful pact was sealed. He also gave me another money pouch from his burgeoning coffers. My protests that I had already been amply rewarded were in vain.

My first visit was to Lindisfarena to bid farewell to the kindly abbot. Not that he took kindly to my consigning the *Vita* without first having shown it to him.

"Forgive my thoughtlessness, Father Abbot, but unless I am

mistaken, King Aldfrith will be eager to show it to you and many others."

"Is that immodesty, my son? Our Lord teaches that humility should be the righteous path. It is God who provides us with our talents and guides our hands."

"Ay, Father, Amen."

He smiled and asked the same question about my plans as the monarch.

"I have been granted land in Ériu; I will take my family there."

"Not without King Aldfrith's permission." His voice was stern.

"The king has consented."

He, too, looked sorrowful, saying,

"It is our loss."

A thought struck me,

"Father Abbot, I am now a wealthy man. Would you consider selling me the black horse that bore me to Melrose?"

He hesitated but perhaps it was the eagerness on my face that convinced him. When he named his price, I doubled it,

"Half for the horse and half for the abbey, Father,"

"Bless you, my son."

Wisely he accompanied me to collect my steed, thus avoiding any unpleasantness with the stable monk. It was evident to the pair of them, from the nuzzling and whinnying that the animal was as fond of me as I of it.

I rode across the causeway feeling like a king myself, but one without burgeoning coffers. On the ride home I reflected on how well the day had gone and how soon I would take my family and both horses to Ériu.

"Whoever first coined the expression *parting is sweet sorrow* might well have been referring to my farewells with Nerian and his family. The fellow ranked alongside his deceased brother and Cuthbert in my heart and through the shroud of barely repressed tears, we left Riding with me glancing one last time at Edwy's Cross. Little did I imagine, with my Edwy, aged four, sitting in front of me astride my steed, that I would see Nerian again in the happiest of circumstances but that was to be many years into the future.

For the purposes of this chronicle, I will sweep over the intervening years, the most contented of my life. I found a fine mare to mate with my stallion, thus began my new life as a horse breeder: the most renowned in southern Ériu. Sherlaith bore me another son, who I named Cuthbert—for obvious reasons. My father, as Sherlaith's said he would, set up a successful leather-working business and the two men became drinking companions.

I fell in love with my adopted country and, although finding God in every rock and wildflower, I still made time to attend the Ardfinnan church and befriend the priest, with whom I had long and fruitful discussions about Christianity. With him, I fulfilled a long-standing ambition, taking Lugaid with us, we rode as far as the River Shannon to visit the monastery of Clonmacnoise, where the monks accorded me the privilege of entering their library and admiring the beautifully crafted volumes. The illustrations, so luminous and splendid, left me agape with wonder. However, in every single case, I felt that I would have made a better binding.

The years passed in this pleasant manner until one day in the early summer of 698 AD, a messenger arrived in Ardfinnan seeking *Master Aella, the Leather-worker.* He bore a message from Abbot Eadberht, which failed to explain why but made clear that my presence was required at the planned opening of Cuthbert's coffin on Lindisfarena. The old monk begged me to make all haste. This I did, taking Edwy with me, he now a lad of eleven winters, and having prevailed upon me to travel with his new horse, a gift of mine. He wished to see his native Northumbria, of which he had the vaguest memories.

The crossing was calm and steady, which was a fortune for us and the skittish animals whilst our ride to Hexham was uneventful but tiring. I stopped there more to give the youth and our beasts a rest, but with the fulfilled hope of finding my carver in good health. From him, I purchased for Edwy a footed cross in jet, so that he should be protected like his mother. I bought another one in ivory, had it wrapped and tucked it away. I think Edwy's brought him some good fortune at once as I will explain. First, however, we stopped at Edwy's Cross and I told my son the tale of why I had erected this monument and how his namesake, my best friend, had fallen to a Pictish arrow before my eyes.

"I hate the Picts!" Edwy said with such a tone of bitterness that even I was shocked.

"Well, be that as it may, let's find Edwy's brother who's a good friend."

The huge waterwheel was turning when we arrived, so I knew Nerian was at work. We were met at the gate by a shy smiling creature, a bonny girl of Edwy's age.

I dismounted and crossing to her in three strides, bent down level with her face and kissed her brow and said, to her wide-eyed wonderment,

"You'll be Osythe, my goddaughter."

She flung her arms around my neck,

"Uncle Aella!" she cried, hugging me tightly, "Father will be so happy!"

I pressed the package into her hand,

"This is for you, my dear girl. Oh, and this is my son, Edwy," he had tied up the horses and joined us.

Her shyness returned but Edwy took her in his embrace for

the first of many times and like me, kissed her on the brow. She hugged him, too.

"Aella! Is it you?" Eawynn emerged from her house, hands white with flour and she wiped them on her apron.

"It is I! My goodness, how Osythe has grown!" I turned to smile at my goddaughter, but she had vanished and I had lost my son to her in more ways than one.

"Come into the mill!" Eawynn didn't need to encourage me.

I became covered in flour as I embraced my friend: much to the cackling amusement of Osythe and Edwy. Nerian amazed me by saying,

"Have you seen Aella?"

"But I am here!" Again, to the accompaniment of unfettered laughter.

Nerian busied himself stopping the grinding by shutting off the flow, then led me into his house to meet the new addition to the family: a two-year-old boy, my namesake.

Downcast, I muttered,

"What a fool I am, I should have known," then in a louder voice, "I'll bring *his* gift on my return."

"There's no need for gifts!"

The couple spoke as one, but I meant to ignore them and picking up little Aella, showered them with heartfelt compliments.

Of course, we stayed to eat but then passed the night in my old house, although Eawynn insisted on bringing dry, aired bedding. As Edwy and I lay half-asleep in my marriage bed, his sleepy voice pleaded,

"Father is it necessary that I come to Lindisfarena with you?"

"Don't you want to see the island and the king and all?"

"Well, ay, but—"

"But you're smitten by Osythe, tell it true! Ow!"

A sharp elbow reminiscent of his mother's dug me in the ribs.

"What! Too near the bone for you, was it?" I laughed and had to fight off a writhing, wrestling boy under the covers.

When his energy was spent and he was pinned down by my grip, he confessed,

"I suppose I *do* like Osythe, she's a fair maid and she's fun to be with."

"Ah, *fun*, is she?" I mocked and set off the writhing again. "ah, *fair*, is she?"

That was enough to make him give in. His eyes were heavy after a long, emotional day.

"You'd better get some sleep, my lad," I said pointlessly as his breathing was already deep and even. I lay for a while, listening to him inhale and exhale, wondering why on earth the monks wanted to open Cuthbert's coffin. Instead, I found repose thinking of the honour of having my name given to Nerian and Eawynn's son.

The next day, I introduced Edwy to my fishermen friends before we crossed the causeway. The stable monk at the abbey was overjoyed to be reunited temporarily with my black *Midnight*.

"Ah, you settled on a fine name, come, Midnight, I'll brush you down, my beauty."

I swear my horse had much to say to the cheery monk.

Abbot Eadberht blessed and praised Edwy, recommending him to prayer.

"Father Abbot, it is good to see you again, but I am curious. Why do you wish to open my friend's coffin?"

The elderly monk smiled and evaded the question, preferring to answer with a compliment, in this way:

"Ah, Master Aella, you, who wrote the magnificent tome,

Vita Sancti Cuthberti, should know better than anyone!" This mystified me, frankly. "By the way, the volume is King Aldfrith's pride and joy and he shows it to all visiting dignitaries. Mind you, as Abbot, I think he should be a little less proud!"

I chuckled but frowned, still perplexed,

"Father, I confess my ignorance in such matters. Why must you open the coffin?"

The abbot smiled patiently and assumed an awestruck expression.

"Aella, since your departure, the blessed Cuthbert has performed so many miracles that no-one can deny his sanctity. We seek incontrovertible proof for the Holy Father and the Curia—you see, saints are not corrupt like other people and so, their bodies do not decay but remain intact. We wish to see the state of Cuthbert."

I shuddered involuntarily at the thought of gazing upon my dead friend eleven years after his death. But that was what I was being invited to do, I think it was an honour accorded to Cuthbert's biographer. Edwy refused to come into the crypt and I cannot blame him, because the cavernous room with the flickering candlelight and the distorted shadows cast by the tapers was enough to unman a seasoned warrior, even before the monks withdrew the coffin from the shrine, placed it on a trestle and prised off the lid. The king, abbot, priors, monks and I crowded around the wooden casket.

The horror of seeing the hair, beard and nails grown long, was surpassed by the wonder of observing the undecayed face and body—or *incorrupt* as the monks insisted on chorusing.

"A miracle! A miracle! they cried.

The abbot called for silence and decorum before pronouncing,

"Sire, Brothers, friends, before us we have indisputable

proof if ever we needed it, that the blessed Cuthbert is indeed a saint. I declare him *Saint Cuthbert of Lindisfarena.*"

"Amen!" chorused the monks.

The king whispered in my ear,

"I do believe, Master Aella, that the fine Gospel beside the saint is your work, is it not?"

"Ay, Sire," I murmured, proud that Cuthbert's Gospel lay as incorrupt as the corpse.

Outside the crypt, I made a fateful decision, calling Edwy to me and daring to present him to the king.

"Ah, so this is young Edwy," King Aldfrith smiled, "we have an agreement, do we not, Master?"

Of course, I was obliged to agree.

"My idea," continued the monarch, "is to anticipate our arrangement, given that the young man is already here. What say you, Edwy?"

"Ay, Sire, I'd like that!" piped the young rascal.

"Master Aella?" queried the king.

A wise man never gainsays his ruler, "As you wish, My Lord."

"Good, I will treat Edwy as if he were a son of mine."

The king was true to his word, and when he was older, Edwy received lands and titles. But as I cantered back to Riding Mill bearing a gift for little Aella, I thought nought of such possibilities, but rather of the wherefores of Edwy's keenness to remain in Babbanburgh. I am quick-witted and my boy did not fool me, I reckoned he wished to stay at court to be nearer Osythe. And I was proved right when some years later, news of his betrothal to her reached Ardfinnan. Later still, they produced a son and another named Aella greeted the Northumbrian daylight.

As part of life's infinite cycle, sorrowful events intersperse these joys. But a few months after the opening of Cuthbert's coffin, Abbot Eadberht departed this world. I believe that he planned for, and succeeded in hearing about, Cuthbert's canonisation before his death. Six years later, King Aldfrith went to war with the Picts and my Edwy fought beside him and was one of the warriors who helped the wounded king find refuge from the field of Ebberston in a cavern, called to this day *Elfrid's Hole* by the local folk. The king died in December 704 of his wound.

I am grown old but live every day with my eyes filled with beholding wonders as Cuthbert taught me, I quote his words:

'Behold the lilies of the field, see how they grow! Their growing is your growing, Aella, their fading you share. Become one with the lily, my friend, and you do not become less, but more.'

I have forever treasured these words and am humbled to have been the writer of the *Vita Sancti Cuthberti.*

THE END

Dear reader,

We hope you enjoyed reading *Heaven in a Wild Flower*. Please take a moment to leave a review, even if it's a short one. Your opinion is important to us.

Discover more books by John Broughton at https://www.nextchapter.pub/authors/john-broughton

Want to know when one of our books is free or discounted? Join the newsletter at http://eepurl.com/bqqB3H

Best regards,

John Broughton and the Next Chapter Team

ABOUT THE AUTHOR

John Broughton was born in Cleethorpes Lincolnshire UK in 1948: just one of the post-war baby boom. After attending grammar school and studying to the sound of Bob Dylan he went to Nottingham University and studied Medieval and Modern History (Archaeology subsidiary). The subsidiary course led to one of his greatest academic achievements: tipping the soil content of a wheelbarrow from the summit of a spoil heap on an old lady hobbling past the dig. He did actually many different jobs while living in Radcliffe-on-Trent, Leamington, Glossop, the Scilly Isles, Puglia and Calabria. They include teaching English and History, managing a Day Care Centre, being a Director of a Trade Institute and teaching university students English. He even tried being a fisherman and a flower picker when he was on St. Agnes island, Scilly. He has lived in Calabria since 1992 where he settled into a long-term jobat the University of Calabria teaching English. No doubt his lovely Calabrian wife Maria stopped him being restless. His two kids are grown up now, but he wrote books for them when they were little. Hamish Hamilton and then Thomas Nelson published 6 of these in England in the 1980s. They are now out of print. He's a granddad now and happily the parents wisely named his grandson Dylan. He decided to take up writing again late in his career. When teaching and working as a translator you don't really have time for writing. As soon as he stopped the translation work, he resumed writing in 2014. The fruit of that decision was his first historical novel, *The Purple Thread* followed by *Wyrd of the Wolf*. Both are set in his favourite Anglo-Saxon period. His third and fourth novels, a two-book set, are *Saints and Sinners* and its sequel *Mixed Blessings* set on the cusp of the eighth century in Mercia and Lindsey. A fifth *Sward and Sword* will be published soon and is about the great Earl Godwine. Creativia Publishing have released *Perfecta Saxonia* and *Ulf's Tale* about King Aethelstan and King Cnut's empire respectively. In May 2019, they published *In the Name of the Mother*, a sequel to *Wyrd of the Wolf*. Creativia/Next Chapter also published *Angenga* a time-travel novel linking the ninth century to the twenty-first. This novel inspired John Broughton's latest venture, a series of six stand-alone novels about psychic investigator Jake Conley, whose retrocognition takes him back to Anglo-Saxon times. Next Chapter Publishing scheduled the first of these, *Elfrid's Hole* for publication at the end of October 2019. The second, is *Red Horse Vale* and the third, *Memory of a Falcon*. The fourth is *The Snape Ring* and is on pre-sale on Amazon. The fifth, *Pinions of Gold* is under consideration by the same publisher. The last of the series *The Serpent Wand* is also under consideration.

The author's next project is to create this 'pure' Anglo-Saxon series about Saint Cuthbert.

Printed in Great Britain
by Amazon

27634240R10138